Thomas Nield

Oliver Cromwell

Lord Protector of England

Thomas Nield

Oliver Cromwell
Lord Protector of England

ISBN/EAN: 9783337342180

Printed in Europe, USA, Canada, Australia, Japan

Cover: Foto ©Andreas Hilbeck / pixelio.de

More available books at **www.hansebooks.com**

Oliver Cromwell

LORD PROTECTOR OF ENGLAND

A Drama

THOMAS NIELD.

NEW YORK
THE ARGYLE PRESS
265 CHERRY STREET

PROEM.

See Cromwell here, the Sinai of his age,
Round whom the thunders of Jehovah rolled,
Cloud-clad in the eternal awfulness,
From the grim summit of his crags and peaks
The Infinite vouchsafed the decalogue
Of liberty, to be a basic law,
On which humanity might plant its foot.

A waymark ot the centuries is he.·
The clouds are lifted, and the lurid glare
Of war lends no more carmine to his guise ;
But, in the undimned splendor of his fame,
He stands to-day divinely glorified.
Then doff the shoes of prejudice, and kneel
Before approaching where Jehovah spake.

Dramatis Personae.

CROMWELL,
FAIRFAX,
IRETON, } *Parliamentary Generals.*
LAMBERT,
LUDLOW,
ALLEN, *Adj't General.*
HARRISON, *Major.*
DESBOROW,
WHALLEY,
HAMMOND, } *Parliamentary Colonels.*
PRIDE,
FLEETWOOD,
ST. JOHN, *Lord Chief Justice.*
LENTHALL, *Speaker.*
BRADSHAW,
GROBY,
WHITELOCKE,
WIDDRINGTON, } *Members of Parliament.*
WENTWORTH,
MOORE,
WALTON,
SYDNEY,
BAAS, *French Envoy.*
HIGH SHERIFF.

CHARLES I.
CHARLES II.
DUKE OF GLOSTER, *Son of Charles I*
PRINCESS ELIZABETH, *Daughter of Charles I.*
PRINCE RUPERT, *Nephew of Charles I.*
ASHBURNHAM,
BERKELEY, } *Attendants of Charles I.*
WARWICK,
HYDE, *Attendant of Charles II.*
BISHOP OF LONDON.
DUKE OF BUCKINGHAM.
EARL OF HOLLAND.
GERARD,
VOWELL,
FINCH. } *Loyalist Conspirators.*
HENSHAW,
BILLINGSLEY,
FOX, *A Spy.*
TOMMY, *A Clown.*
Attendants, Commissioners, Judges, Mayors, Soldiers, Citizens.
A WOMAN.

4

OLIVER CROMWELL,

Lord Protector of England.

ACT I.

SCENE I. *The field of Naseby after the battle.* Soldiers *on picket.*

First Soldier. The godly Cromwell girts with glory
old
Britannia's brow.   Yea, and this day will pin
A brave rosette upon her breast.
Second S.   In sooth,
The carnal prigs, who pranked themselves in their
Ungodly pride, have foundered on their fare.
Rupert, the whip, has lost his snapper, and
Will henceforth urge in vain the jaded nag
That bears the king's cause on its bony back.
He will remind himself, while memory lasts,
Of Naseby's field, as where the Lord set down
The foot of his almightiness and said :
" Thus far, proud Prince ! but here thy tether pulls."
  Third S. Marston and Newberry slapped him on the
cheek ;
But Naseby stabs the dare-dog to the heart.—
I wonder what the king is thinking of
To-night.   Belike, his thoughts come thick as dust
On windy days.
  First S.   Ay, thick enough to blind,
Or he had seen the Lord's uplifted hand

Above his head. The evil one has wrought
Confusion in his mind.

Third S.   Then Satan is
Against Beelzebub ; for devil's work
He does for devilish ends.

Second S.   ,   The King of kings
Gives Satan leave to overreach himself,
To have him find what he would gladly lose.
Hence has the arch fiend made the king his dupe,
Whose madness makes his mettle rush to doom
'Neath Retribution's lash.

Third S.   The Ironsides
Have dug a grave full big enough for all
His greed, his tyranny, and papistries.
There but awaits an inquest on the corpse :
A thing to be before the year has bid
Good-by.

Fourth S. [*Approaching*]. An inquest? Half a score
      will get
No inquest, I'll be bound.

Third S.   Why half a score ?

Fourth S. I knocked them in the head ; and day
      will find
Too big a task on hand to ferret out
How every dog received his honest dues.
Mercy would give them all like boon.   To hear
Them groan and beg the drink they cannot get ;
To see them eke their sufferings out and die,
Brings tender tingling into Pity's ear,
And is too much for Mercy to resist,
When one good blow can be a quietus.

Third S. How fine when sympathy and interest
      meet,
Shake hands and kiss each other ! Killing then
Is such a virtuous thing ; and we advance
A step towards heaven in sending one to hell !

Fourth S. The blarney stone was kissed with worm-
wood in
Thy mouth.
First S.   It smacks of cowardice to kill
Who cannot do us further harm.   'Tis but
To kill a worm.   And who would count that brave ?
Fourth S. What want we here, except to kill who
have
No right to live ? who are the burden, bane
And blasting of the land ? who would but live
To kill us for our ruth, or ram our throats
With an ungodly king, who has the stench
Of Rome upon his skirts, and England's blood
Upon his hands ?   Best done when cheapest done,
And done most thoroughly, what all want done
Who would not have our liberties undone.
Second S. We are the sword of Justice, whose it is
To kill, not spare.
First S.   Yet something in one's blood
Makes loth to shed, in simple wantonness,
The blood of Englishmen.   Tis bad enough
When battle's frenzy urges us.
Fourth S.   Ay, but
Who knows what mongrel rabble serves the king—
Bogtrotting Irishman, and Scot, and French,
And Englishmen who shamed the English name?
And papists all—sworn to un-English us,
With their fantastic and ungodly ways,
Or kill us, English as we are, in blood,
In heart, and all that gives good savor to
The name.   Ay, one or other is the sauce
They offer us.   We must be slaves or die.
The first, an Englishman can never be ;
The second, never do till he extorts
The price in blood for blood.   So here they are
To take it.   Let them pay our price ; as pay

They shall—and ten to one of wastrel stuff—
For what they get. [*A groan from one approaching on*
hands and knees.

  Third S.   Who comes?
  Royalist Soldier.   An Englishman.
  Second S. Thy English may be but the color of
An adder with a fatal fang. Speak thou—
A friend or foe?
  R. S.   In too ill plight to be
A foe.
  Fourth S. Think not thy plight, if fruitage of
Thy own misdeeds, can shelter thee.
  R. S.   Distress
Is plea that must prevail with English blood.
  Third S. In sooth, thou seemest in too dreadful
   plight
To be a dreadful foe.   But hadst thou done
Thy will, we were as thou and thou as we.
Then hadst thou been as chirk and chuff, I ween,
As a fat goose in sight of Christmas-tide.
  R. S. Think thou art me and I am thou, and do
Thou now as thou would'st have me then, and so
Be best thyself, by being what thine own
Best self would be.
  Third S.   Thy tongue, I fear me, is
A ready snare, to take one's nature on
The woman side.
  R. S.   Nay, fear no snare from one
Who shivers on life's farther shore ; nor let
The choler born of general strife make thee
Dispiteous towards a countryman, who asks
Thee but to glove Death's calloused hand.
  Fourth S.   So worse,
If countryman disloyal to the realm,
And so a red-hot traitor to us all,
Whose hand has cramped in holding on our throat.

R. S. Nay, loyal to the king—the head,—and so
To all the body true. [*He falls over and stretches out.*
   Fourth S.   Mercy to thee,
I fear me, were no mercy to the realm.
   First S. Be not at loggerheads about the head,
Which this day's work has taken from the trunk.
Would'st thou a drink ?   [*Stooping down.*
   R. S.   A drink—a drink—a drink.
   First S. Here, take the last I have to serve thy last.
   R. S. [*After drinking*]. Heaven give its best to serve
      thy last !
   First S. [*Rising*]. Nature
Is older than the realm or king, and binds
Us in a broader brotherhood.   Then while
Defenceless suffering lies beside our path,
As Lazarus at the rich man's gate, forbid
That we should be less pitiful than dogs,
Which plied him with their only pharmacy.
   Fourth S. But Nature has a head as well as heart.
   First S. Yet nothing here offends against the head.
Had Charles but more of heart and less of head,
We had been shouting now, God save the king !
Then give we kinghood to the qualities
For lack of which he bids to be unkinged,
Assured that we, by having what he lacks,
Shall gain where he has lost and king the right.
Wend thou in memory to the wanton days
When thou wert wandering with a wayward foot,
And tread again the ins-and-outs that made
Thy life a labyrinth of sin ; then say
If mercy did thee harm, or left the grace
Of God aught poorer by enriching thee.
   Fourth S. Well, give thy charity a stretch.   'Twill
      cost thee nought.
   First S. [*Stooping*]. Death makes us kin ; and
      doubly so

In English cloth.   It were not meet for me
To weigh thy sins, who have my own ; and steel
My heart, which is by nature hard ; or to
Denounce and label thee for doom,
When Judge there is, in whose impartial scales
Our shrinkages will shew.   What can I more
To smooth thy exit hence ?
  R. S.   Thy ruth for one
Who earned it not will give thee weight at last,
When tested by the balance of the Judge.
God pay that ruth on earth by giving one
To help my brother should he meet like stress.
 · *First S.* Thy brother ?   Prythee, man, how so ?
 R. S.   The tongue
Of Rumor hath it that he took to arms
Against his gracious Majesty.   Kind Heaven
Above knows how he fares to-night.   Oh, sad
It is to have a brother traitor to
His king !   Yet would I have him spared, in hope
He may return to loyalty.   Or if
The tug of death be on, Heaven send him friends.
 First S. Thy brother's name ?
 R. S.   John Summerfield.
 First S.   From where ?
 R. S. From Thame.
 First S. Thou dost not say !   Thy name ?
 R. S.   Jerome.
 First S. Heaven save us !   Thee Jerome ?   And I
  am John—John Summerfield, of Thame.
 R. S.   Heaven ! can it be ?
Methought a something brotherly was in
Thy heart, suspecting not a brother's hand.
This makes my hard earth-pillow turn to down :
Yet not without a thorn, to know that thou
Art in so bad a cause.   For hope is fled
From England while her king is smitten by

Their hands who ought to do him reverence. Nay,
What hope have they who do him this despite
Should death find treason's brand upon their brow ?

First S. We owe the king but what his deeds have
earned,
Which deeds are ill—and pay but like for like.

R. S. But he is none the less our lawful king,
Whom none, except the Judge of all, may judge
In lawfulness.

First S. I call the king a man ;
Than which thou would'st not call him more. Admit,
Who is but man, while yet he breaks the laws
Of man, must answer at man's judgment bar.

R. S. A man ; and yet a God-anointed man ;
And hence his will is as the will of God.
Then who are we to say our Maker nay ?

First S. Our Maker ! Does He hellish deeds to serve
His ends ? Bids he a Charles be tyrant ; stamp
His foot upon the laws he swore to keep ;
Distress the land to overfeed a few ;
Outlie the Devil with a pious twang ;
Ay, put the very Devil to the blush ?
Away thy spider-woven quillets that
Would hold his honor to the flagstaff whose
Vile deeds invoke the winds to tatter it.
No crown can sanctify his villainies.

R. S. To mete out chastisement to villains is
No villainy ; and villain's villains are
A Fairfax, Cromwell, and such like.

First S. By him
I serve, thou art unbrothered from this hour—
Un-Englished—alienated—made a nought
To me, save as I can imagine thee
A something to dispatch.

R. S. Ah, John, there is
Too little to dispatch to pay thee for

A blow !   But let me die a score of times,
Though by a score of brothers' hands, to serve
My king, rather than save the fag-end of
A life by failing him who has the web.
First S. Then die if thou art mad as that ! [*Stepping back.*] But let
Thy poisoned lip dare brother me no more.
I rue me of the ruth already shown.
To think that thou should'st make the king a Baal !
Should'st call the godly Cromwell villain, when
A paring of his finger-nail were worth
A score such kings ! Thou art a Hottentot
In soul ; while I am English through and through.
Death never did a better thing than when
He saved my father's ears from hearing thee ;
Nor life a worse, than when he let me hear.
   Fourth S. If thou art squeamish I can stop his prate.
                   [*Raising his musket.*
   First S. Hold ! Let us not forestall the hand of
     Death.
   Fourth S. We have forestalled it when we had less
     prate.
In this black mouth [*holding up the muzzle of his musket*]
     there is a tongue that tells
Our mission, which is a forestalling one.
Malignants have to die or live to kill.
Allow them life, we sanction our own death.
He would not spare us with a snaphance cocked.
   First S. His end is near and needs no help from thee.
Climb not a falling tree to bring it down,
Nor step on one, when down, to keep it there.
                    [*Exeunt.*

Scene II. King Charles *pacing the floor in a room of Newark Castle.*

Charles. Unlucky stars are in conjunction, and
The ill-breeding midnight of ill fate
Has brought the wraith of destiny to haunt
My mind. The tempest flaps its wings of wrath
Above the columned powers that held the throne.
That *held.* Alas! The tense is in the past—
The deaf, dead past. Those powers are low, amid
The ruins of whose cornices and shafts
My shattered majesty is prone, until
Myself seems other than myself. Avaunt!
Be laid, thou ghostly moodiness! I have
A fit of mental rheum, which films the eye
And ill befits anointed royalty.
Insensate nature's equinoxes have
Their place and mission as the left hand of
Beneficence, to fit the woods to wear
The morning gown of spring. And why not, in
This higher sphere, a higher end? A voice
Within me says : Paint not thy landscape by
The light of stars. Yet was I painting on
A cloudy night, with canvas pitchy black.
Arise, O Sun! Awake, my better self!
Look through the gloam of Providence and wait.
Already light is blushing on my thoughts,
Flushed by the rosy laughter of the dawn. —
Heaven sends a purge for humors in the blood ;
From which comes nausea that affects the head.
That head is brain, eye, ear, nose, mouth, in one :
Which make it necessary to the trunk.
Hence must I be the thinker for the realm,
To solve this problem of calamity.
My eye must see where every danger lurks ;
My ear must hear when'er it stirs a foot ;

My nostril scent it when it changes place ;
My mouth blow tally-ho to swoop the pack.—
Ah, me ! The problem still is on the slate ;

[*Sitting down.*

And, like a wit-dazed schoolboy, I behold
The figures that outstare me as they had
An idiot's eyes. My armies have been as
The summer clouds. My strongholds crumbled at
The cannon's mouth. My friends proved icicles,
Which melted as the breath of treason warmed.
Now I am caitiff to a caitiff crew,
Whose brutishness is gloating o'er my plight.
Thus there remains my solitary self—
My naked self ; more naked than when born.
Myself? Then I have but myself to trust ;
Nor other e'er was worthy of like trust.
My *naked* self ? Then I must clothe myself ;
Wrap the broad mantle of my majesty
About me ; breed devices worthy of
A king, to counterbuff the cunning of
My foes, then make them stagger with the blows
I deal. And stagger shall they, every one,
When Retribution lets me grasp his lance.
O Justice ! slowly lifts thy arm ; but when
It falls, it falls a flaming thunderbolt.

Enter Prince RUPERT.

Sure king had never greater need of friends,
Nor greater lack of friends to serve his need.

Rupert. Friends are not few ; but, like your Majesty,
They are sore beaten by the present stress ;
For 'tis their fall that lays your fortunes low.

C. True, nominally I have friends ; friends who
Appreciate my smile, and use it as
They might my coat—to keep them warm ; and friends
Who, with my interests on their back, were sure

To stumble to my lasting loss. Such friends
Would serve me best when farthest off.

    R.   Pray put
Not me in such a catalogue ; for not
An atom of my being but would rouse
To slap the base insinuation on
The cheek. 'Tis true, I served you **when** you smiled.
But smiles were none had I not served you well.
Nay, every smile I got was doubly earned.
Say that I stumbled : had all stumbled like
Myself, from greatest lord to meanest churl
Had shewn, ere this, a supple knee.

    C.   A zeal
There is that has no ear when Prudence warns ;
But with infatuated force it speeds,
And leaps the precipice whose depth it would
Not see ; as if its blindness might avert
Its doom.

    R.   And other zeal there is—a zeal
That beards exigencies and tears them limb
From limb. Such was the zeal I spent to serve
Your cause ; a zeal too great, too true, too good,
For your ingratitude to measure it
And grant its dues.

    C.   Who wrote, in running-hand,
The tragedy of Marston Moor ? You know.
Who skinned the left hand of the rebel force
At Naseby, then, not many lances length,
Stood by, with sword well scabbarded, and let
The foe cut down the prop that held our hopes ?
You know. Who held the keys of Bristol in
His hand, with charge to keep them as he kept
His life, yet at a cock-crow shook and gave
Them up ? You know. Ill fare is that to feed
A prince's boast.

    R.   A loyal heart, and arm

That serves a king—though falling short of that
At which they aim—should find an ægis in
His gratitude. Much more should he whose one
Sole fault, if fault it be, is this—he served
Too well. Say failure was my forte. Share you
The blame whose eyes have seen it not till now,
But who requited with repeated trusts.
But fail I did not : and did egoism leave
Your honesty ungagged, you so would say.
That I at Marston Moor did all that's worth
The boasting of, you know. What odds to me,
Or what the derogation of my fame,
That others lagged behind ? That what was won
At Naseby I was winner of, you know.
What odds, what blame, that I could not transfuse
My soul ? That I in Bristol could but cower
Above the black and cooling embers of
Your cause, you know. What gain to starve a town
And give its carcass to the dogs, to prove
One's stubbornness ? That thus, when free from clogs
Of lumbering laggards, I compelled success,
And failed but when you bade me climb the heights
Of the impossible, you know. And yet
You raise the ghost of Bristol to remind
Me that my feeble force foiled not a host,
Forgetful of my gallantry when it
Was bristled o'er with men. If few might hold,
What glory that I took it many-manned ?
Your memory ought to shame your tongue to tell
The better as it tells the worse. For I
Am not distilling secrets in your ear.

    C. Yet you possess the art of striking an
Occasion on the hip, or you had not
Presumed to harry me with insolence.   •
But mark, young prince : capricious Fortune, who
Has shorn our royalty and oiled thy tongue,

May shear thee yet, and give thy mouth a gag.
Think'st thou that God, whose substitute I am,
Is deaf, and will not vindicate His own
Against thy railleries?   I tell thee nay ;
But He will follow thee to any nook
Of earth, and flaunt thy follies in thy face,
Until thou call'st upon the past to give
Thee back thy words, that thou mayst triturate
Them into sheer unmeaningness, and sink
Them, slime-deep, in oblivion's grass-green depths.
Yea, He will vindicate me as Himself.

 R. Perchance I wear the slippers of a king,
As you the shoes.   And, by my troth, I would
Not make exchange ; for you, to-morrow, may
But be the shadow of a king, while I
Possess the substance of a prince.   Indeed,
I am to-day more prince than you are king.
Thus am I vindicated more than you,
And have less discount of divinity.

 C. O callow youth ! to have a blind eye to
The fact that crooked lanes oft come out right
At last, and straight ones dead against a wall.
When darkness broods, it makes us realize
All-present power and reach beyond ourselves
To grasp Omnipotence.   Our weakness thus
Becomes our strength ; our darkness, light.   Prepare
Thee, then, to hear that Charles of England sits
On England's throne, more firmly rooted for
The wrestling of the winds that bluster now.
And when thou hear'st, recall thou, and repent
Of this thy barbed impertinence, and bid
Thy Judgment sentinel at Duty's post.
So shall thy folly turn to good account,
And serve thee as misfortune serves my turn.

 R. Nay, your centrifugal ingratitude,
Which drives away your friends, will leave you lone ;

For e'en devotion, fastened by a score
Of ties, stands not forever, hat in hand,
To do the bidding of a thankless king.
There is your blindness ; there the bane in all
You say and do.   Brave hearts pour out their blood,
And you reproach them that they have no more.

    C. As sure as God is God and I am king,
If thou wilt stay on England's soil thy tongue
Shall cost thee dear.

     R.   Oh, bugbear oath !   As sure
As you are king, whose tongue is all your head ;
The all of Charles ; the final morsel of
A king ; a bit of quivering flesh, which, like
A snake's tail, squirms because the other end
Is scotched !   Think you I fear a cast-off king,
Who in his heyday leaned upon my arm,
And threats because I cannot longer bear
The dead weight of his helplessness ?   Who, think
You, waits to see you nod ?   This garrison,
Which treats you as a boy his broken kite ?
An Essex—Fairfax—Cromwell ; they whose swords
Will thirst until they drink your blood ? or a
Mad Parliament, which makes itself the stake
Of War's relentless game ?   Your lightning is
The other side the earth.   Your thunder sole
Remains.

    C.   As thou hast been the wormwood in
My cup, so now its bitterest dregs are in
Thy flippant and malicious fluency.
Well, let me drink it if it be His will
Who makes both wormwood and the roses grow.

    R. It shews one's stomach when we sicken at
The truth.   But most commendable is this
Politic piety—to yield yourself
A victim to necessity.   Had but
A tithe of this complaisance nimbused you

Upon the throne, you were not kenneled now,
With such a set of keepers as are here.

 C. Go thou, and leave my sight forevermore,
Nor set again a foot on this fair soil.

 R. Command the sun to shine, and me to go.
Both will obey.   And fear not my return.
The freed bird will not seek its former cage.   [*Exeunt.*

Scene III. *On the street near Westminster.   A crowd
of* Apprentices.

 First Apprentice. God save the king !
  Second A.   Give us a head.
  Third A.   'Twould stun
A dozen lords to tell us whether he
Be head or tail, the way he wags.
  Fourth A.   Bring back
The king and good old times.
  Fifth A.   The good old times
Are buried five years deep.   It's been but strife
And ill-luck since he left.
  Shouts.   A commoner !
There goes a commoner.   Pelt him with stones.
God save the king !   The king !   We want the king !
  Sixth A. I'm sick of wasting blood ; and English
   blood
To boot : and goodness knows what for.
  Third A.   Belike,
You want black puddings by the yard.
  Fifth A.   Where *is*
The king ?
  Third A. Shut in a box, for aught I know,
And fed on lollipop.
  Fourth A.   I wish he were
But back to share with us ; for we have had
More loll than pop.

Sixth A.   We never had a chance
The match of this to count our ribs ; and, king
Away, we soon may have no ribs.
 Third A.   What boots
A king, to eat fat dinners and be coached
About, with full-fed flunkies at his heels?
We have too much to do to feed ourselves.
 Sixth A. There, take a raw beefsteak thyself.
     [Slapping him on the mouth.
 Fifth A.   The place
Beefsteaks are always meant to fit.
 Third A.   Here's at
Thee.   *[Striking. Several lay hold of him.*
 Fourth A. Watch thy hide or thou may'st have no
   hide
To watch.
 Second A. No king, no head ; no head, no tail ;
No head or tail, no anything.
 Seventh A.   'Tis time
This everlasting dilly-dally—ay,
And fiddle-faddle—of the Commons had
An end.   Their wind will fill no dinner-pot
With broth.
 The Mob. Ho for the Commons! Make them vote.
The Commons! on! The Commons! Tie their tongues
And make them vote.
   [Rushing to the door of the House of Commons.
 Shouts.   Open the door.   Open,
Or we will splinter it to shoe-pegs.   Bring
Some paving-stones, and we will find a way.
     [The door is broken open.
 The Mob [Entering]. Vote! Vote!
 Speaker [Leaving the chair].   The members
   must be free, or what
They do is void.
 A Voice.   Full free they are to do

As we demand ; as do they must.

                  [*The Speaker is pushed into the chair.*

Second V.   No tricks
To-day, but work.

   First V.   What answer has the house
To our petition ?

Sp.   As to that, the house
Has had the matter in advisement, and
Desires to act as in its wisdom suits
The gravity—

   First V.   Oh, no palaver now !
You mean that nought is done. Then we demand
That you undo what yesterday you did.
You dubbed us traitors who demand the king.
We bid you wipe your hand across the lie.

   Second V. The king must be restored. So much we
        want ;
And, by our right arm, so much we will have.

   Shouts. We mean it, word for word. Give back the
        king
And peace ! Give us the king and work ! The king !
Peace ! Work ! The king and good old times ! We
        wont
Have nay. Vote ! Vote !

   Sp.   What must we vote ?

   Shouts.   To have
The king come back.

   Sp.   Aught else ?

   First V.   To have him come
With safety, freedom, honor, as befits
A king.

   Sp.   Now vote you, gentlemen, on both
Of these, as pleases you.

   Second V.   As pleases *us,*
Or you will be mispleased.

   Members [*Shouting*]. Aye !

Others.   No.

Sp.   The ayes
Prevail.

　　A Voice.   But which way have you voted?

Sp.   To
Restore the king; so hie you home and keep
The peace.

　　Shouts.   Three cheers for bonny Charles, the king.
                              [*Cheers.   Exeunt.*

SCENE IV.   King CHARLES *at Woburn, in a room of the
                        Castle.*

　　Charles [*Alone*]. The tide is turned, and I am with
        the flood.
A few more shallows passed, I shall be moored.
My hand must hold the helm and mark the tide,
Keeping my craft mid-stream.   For but myself
Can manage what so much concerns myself.
This herd has played the bull and gored me sore;
But wit shall ring it yet and make it do
My bid.   For so it is: brutes wanton with
Their strength till man subdues, and armies with
A king until his wit awakes.   *Awakes?*
That word has touched a fact.   With dormant wit,
I pitted force to force, and trusted not
Myself; an almost fatal fault!   One kingly head
Is more than armies in the field, by so
Much as divinity surpasses what
Is commonplace and gross.   But say adieu
To that.   At length I am awake.   This head
Shall master all the masters of the field.
Indulgent Time! spread out the canvas of
Thy opportunities, that I may etch
My purposes on thy expanse, and shew

The world what glory crowns the genius of
A king.

Ashburnham [*Entering*]. How fares your gracious
    Majesty?

   C. God bless thee, Jack, for such a gracious word!
My spring is meadow-green. Blue skies o'erhead
Have clouds of nugget gold and silver ore.
The winds are warm, and welcome as the queen's
First kiss. The red streams of my life are flush
With April rains, and the imprisoned buds
Of promise burst their bars. O, Jack! it tones
One's courage up to hear the linnets of
His hope.

   A.   'Tis more than *aqua vitæ* to
A man to find you in so gay a mood;
For none too gay, if I can read the times.

   C. Thine eye, Jack, were a credit to a king.

   A. Inside the show, I would not miss to see
The lion eat his keepers. Hence I watch
The movements in the cage.

   C.   Thy fun is as
A finger-prod between the ribs. It starts
The owls of melancholy from their roost.

   A. And there is nought to call them back, while these
Curmudgeon generals dill-down in their fear.
It is a hybrid show—a cross between
A funeral and a mask—to see the way
They twitch and jerk, and yawn and scratch their heads,
Get up and strut, and then sit down again.
Now Fairfax looks at Ireton, who returns
His gaze; then both at Cromwell, fidgeting,
With an interrogative eye, solemn
By turns as fifty monks in Lent, and then
As wrathful as a baited bear. They feel
Themselves enmeshed, and want a king to cut
The mesh.

C.   The caitiffs will abide my time ;
And they may thank their stars if several heads
Adorn not Holborn Hill.

A.   In sooth, it were
A goodly sight for the apprentices
Who swarmed the Commons, clamoring for their king.
A decent batch of heads would feed their hearts
Like mortar, as their loyalty clung close
As ivy to the throne.

C.   Ah, Jack ! were I
In London now, this phantom army would
Evanish in a week.   But Patience points
Me to the clock of luck, whose midnight hour
Is near ; and patiently I shall await
Its stroke.

A.   That is a comfortable view —
A pillow where your head may lie on down,
While plaguy thoughts give place to pleasant dreams.
There rest your Majesty till Fortune taps
You on the arm and becks you to the throne.

C. What answer, thinkest thou, should I return,
When these recalcitrants come suing next
For terms ? as so I understand is their
Intent.   But that I need not ask ; for thou
Hast kingliness of soul that makes thee half
A king.

A.   Beshrew me, I should make them feel
That 'twas a royal and offended hand
They sought ; and so 'twould breed a chill behind
The neck.

C.   Just like thee, honest Jack !   I will
Remember thee and all thy worthy speech.
Thy counsel earns embalmment from thy king ;
For thou hast ever counseled to his mind :
And ne'er was counsel needed more than now :
Leave me alone, and I will weigh it well.

                                        [*Exit Ashburnham.*

One is not poor while such a friend remains.
His intuitions are a telescope
That pierces the galactic circle of
Affairs and shows the remedy for ills ;
While others move like blind men, with the learned
Dog *Chance* to lead.   There is withal a plague
Of poltroonry and weakness everywhere :
An admonition to be more myself.   [*A knock.*
Ah, who comes now?   [*Enter Sir John Berkeley.*]   You
     seem a picture of
The day, or of a man whose dinner fits
His stomach to its full circumference.

   B. 'Twould cheer the rifted heart of Grief to see
Your Majesty in such a playful mood.

   C. Man's circumstances make his moods ; and mine,
Now gibbous as the moon, are waxing fast
And promising the full.

   B.   And faster than
We see with naked eye ; enough to set
Our hopes agog.   Your Majesty has here
A draft of proposition mutually
Prepared by parliament and army, which
Will be presented as a basis for
Your restoration to the throne.   And such
It is as well may make your blood bound in
A rapturous cataract.

             [*Hands the paper to Charles, who reads.*
   C.   That which concerns
The parliament may be allowed ; as well
The small adjustments by disfranchisement,
With lesser items.   But I must object
To divers other hard conditions, which
Accord not with the honor of a king,
And which they would not venture to propose
Did they in honest faith desire to close
With me.   They seek but an excuse for deeds

They cannot justify, and think me blind
Enough, or weak enough, to lay my head
Upon their block.   But I am as the sun,
Whose disk they cannot hide with one small hand
Of craft, and, citadeled in royalty,
Beyond their power to breach.   [*Charles still reading.*
   B.   Did they ask less,
I should believe them falser than they are ;
For when the heart is tensioned by success,
It does not sound in low and abject notes,
Except when tampered with to please the ear.
Thank God they strike so weak a string, and get
So little where they hope for much.   Sure crown,
So nearly lost, was ne'er so cheaply saved.
They ask but little that may not inure
To your advantage, with a quirk of wit ;
The wit that is indigenous to your
Exuberant mind.
   C.   Some exigencies tweak
The nose of Wit, and laugh in mockery of
Our helplessness.   It calls for more than wit
To save the head when drops the axe of doom.
Their scheme is this : to make a puppet king,
Without a soul or living arm of power :
A seal to stamp their actions with, and make
Rebellion smirk with my authority.
But they mistake if they regard me as
In penitential mood, content to take
Such flagellations as their spleen would give.
The nerve of royalty remains—the strong
And ineradicable consciousness
Of my anointing from above, which makes
Me necessary to the realm I hold in trust
To Him who made it mine inheritance.
Note the humiliation they demand :
That I, with bandaged eyes, subscribe to have

Them do their will on seven most trusted friends.
What more could they, except to ask *my* life?
Sure never king did leave the summit of
His majesty to kneel so low.   Shall I
Be first, and by consent?   The axe that took
Those heads would graze my skin and leave a scar
That time's mutations never could outgrow.
Then shall the frown of this capricious hour
Make me unmindful of my dignity?
Scath me heaven's thunderbolts, if so I be!

   B. 'Tis but a humor of the passing hour,
Born of the rancor that exhales like mist
From sodden fields, but which will be dispersed
When War has scabbarded his sword, and Peace
Caressed the country into smiles.   But should
Some adverse cause retard, with little strain
Upon your word you may avert the blow,
By banishing the victims of their wrath.

   C. My word is but the echo of my will.
Hence, changing this, the echo too must change.
But not my word, my honor is at stake.
What most concerns me is, thus to concede
That I am squeezed into so close a strait.   [*Reading.*
Nay, still a keener cut than that is here.
They shut the door of Parliament against
My friends, thus branding royalty a crime,
To make me powerless, while they panoply
Themselves in the substantial dignities
Of kingship; which to ask, is insolence
Too diabolical for hell; and which
To give, I must be false to every trust,
Pollute the holiest sanctities of my
Estate, and make my name a byword for
The world to spit upon.   No!   Take my head,
But take it with my honor on its brow.

   B. In sooth, your Majesty, the whole affair

Will prove a pompous puppet-show, in which
They will but, in imaginary power,
Obey the strings that you will have in hand.
'Twill boot you well to have them strut the stage
And get the hisses of a discontent
That even now is fidgeting.   The foot
Of War has left a wreck behind that will
Not be repaired without some draining of
The country's purse ; when, with the drain, will come
A general blame, redounding to your praise,
Who never did the like.   So will it prove
A counter irritant and work a cure.

   C. Charles Stuart, triply kinged, lie abjectly
At rebels' feet until their blunders bid
Him rise ! That were to ask of me to be
No more myself.   Orion rather shall
Vacate his azure throne, and Death dismount
His horse, and Time put up his scythe, than I
Imperil my prerogative.   And yet [*Reading*].
A deadlier dreg of infamy is in
The cup with which they hope to burn my lip.
Not satisfied to strip the body, they
Would steal eternal treasures from the soul.
Infatuate fanatics !   They would starve
The church ; for they provide no nourishment.
O Berkeley ! In the church eternal hopes
Are shrined.   The church is marrow to us—life,
Light, power.   The church, I say—the *church*, which is
The ark that consecrated hands have borne
Adown the ages in unbroken line ;
Where hovers the shekinah of the truth,
Which guarantees the throne the presence of
Omnipotence.   The king must save the church
As he would keep his throne and save his soul.
No Independent lunacy must be
Allowed ; no Presbyterian bastardy

Be dubbed legitimate ; but she—heaven-born,
The virgin of the Lord—must be preserved,
Inviolable in her purity,
By me, the heaven-appointed guardian of
Her chastity. And think you I shall fail?
First move the pillars of the eternal throne.
How could I yield in this and meet my Judge ?

 B. Most gracious Majesty! the law remains,
A rock against the billows of their rage ;
Nor will it budge in grinding them to spray.
But mark how pregnant is their silence here,
And from that silence auspicate some good.
Silence, when they are tempted so to speak,
Implies an utterness of unconcern
That gives a chance to thumb-and-finger them,
When Fortune's wheel brings round the lucky hour.

 C. I execrate the thought of taking terms
From those who ought to seek me on their knees.
'Tis they, not me, who have to yield. I am
Essential to these kingdoms as the sun ;
And I shall see them glad to kiss my hand.
That answer has a sign and seal within
My heart ; nor can it be revoked. [*Exit Berkeley.*
          Wrong is
A Judas, doomed to die of suicide ;
And here it sees the rope. My honor as
A Christian king—they yet shall feel my hand.
For Newark's contumely, for multiplied
Affronts and harrowings of vicissitude,
Their heads were paltry pay.

 B. [*Re-entering*].   The generals come.
 C. Here let them learn how weak they are.
 B.   To lay
These troubles in the grave of peace, were worth,
Methinks, a funeral costing half your crown.

 C. Not half-a-crown in minted silver, if

In compromise.   'Twere so much thrown away ;
For what we buried would but rise again,
Before the bar of Justice to account.
My right is, everything ; and I shall have
My right.

Enter CROMWELL, IRETON, *and others.*

Cromwell. The parliament and army are
Agreed upon the terms we may present,
With safety to the realm and honor to
Your Majesty, as pledge and guaranty
Of peace.   We come, as representing both,
To learn your pleasure when we bruit the terms.

   C. The terms are known ; hence little breath you need.
   Crom. That gives you season for mature reply;
Which, as you love yourself and we the realm,
May have, I hope, complaisance on its lip.
   C. It *is* mature ; since every fiber of
It is an everlasting principle
Of right.   You ask to immolate,
Upon the altar of assent, seven victims to
Your vengeance ; whose sole fault is having served
Myself, their king, to whom the King of kings
Has made them liege.   Thus would you curse whom
          Heaven
Has blessed, and bless where He has cursed—to prove
How well you love the realm !   Is that not so ?
   Ireton. We ask exclusion of that number from
The general amnesty.
   C.   You bid me turn
The keys of Westminster against my friends !
And so to put a fragment of my crown
On every head that plans to shatter it,
And leave myself the shadow of a king—
A memory, tinseled o'er with nothingness.
What more could you have asked, except my head ?

Yet these, you think, are honorable terms !

 Crom. Five years of war have wrenched the roots of
   things ;
And not till time turns back can we be where
We were. The strife whose bloody foot has left
Its print on every hearth, was not a prank
To fill a holiday. We started with
An object in our eye. Perchance you have
An inkling what it was. Those years have placed
Us well in reach of it. If you, whose hopes
Are dangling from the last thin thread, still snatch
For what is gone, be not astounded that
We hold to what we have so well in hand.

 C. Is gone ? Ah, feeble jeer ! and feebler still
Your boast. You have a blind eye to the facts
To think that aught of my prerogative
Is gone. I still am king, by Heaven's decree,
And these my kingdoms' will ; while you hold but
A phantom by the tail, which will elude
You ere you are aware. Who butcher well
Are not omnipotent.

 B. [*To the king*]. A word. [*They step aside.*] If
   aught
Your Majesty retains of secret power,
Whose whisper is too sacred for my ear,
Think you 'tis wise to trumpet it in theirs?
          [*They return.*

 I. Bethink your Majesty what precipice
Is by your path, nor tempt its vasty depth.
Once o'er, a crown would scarcely break your fall ;
And blood has left a slippery standing-place.

 C. As stands a mountain on a thirsty plain,
And from its cloud-peaks waters all around,
So stand I, and so necessary are
The fruitful rills and rivulets I give.
Remove me, you remove the source of life.

Hence I compassionate the country's plight,
And readily will yield, as Honor gives
Her fair assent, in what forfends her weal.
My jealousy has been that honor to
Defend and the inheritance I hold
In trust. I would be better understood.
Then take my warrant that a woman's heart
Is not more tender than my will. I mean
To serve you as my wisdom prompts. But Time
Takes double toll. The wounds that minutes made
Will take us months to heal ; and years to wreck
Ask years for building up. Then hold ye in
Abeyance these affairs, till I essay
To help your wits. Some day you shall receive
A further word.   [*Exeunt.*
[*To Berkeley.*] What mightinesses these
Brave pigmies make, strutting in stolen boots !
They want my hand to help them out and save
Their necks. And well are they concerned about their
       necks.
They will be more so ere the game is played. [*Exeunt.*

SCENE V.   CHARLES *at Hampton Court, alone.*

Major Legg [*Entering*]. Your Majesty has greater
     gloom than wont—
A gloom that bodes no good to body, while
The mind may grow bewitched and sodden in
Its moods. Look to the credit side of your
Affairs and see a cause for cheerfulness.
Your royalty is round you like a robe.
Your innate greatness is illustrious still.
Your circumstances feed the flame of hope.
Then seat yourself beneath the dais of
Yourself—your philosophic self—gristled
In every limb, and stanch in soul. So shall

The monarch's majesty beseem the orb
That lights the sateilites of state.
   Charles.   Words leave
The lips like oil, yet fail to lubricate
The inward gear. Thank God, you know not what
It is to be a cast-off king ; to sink
Into the quicksands, down from care to care :
To sink, I say, beneath the burdens of
The realm, and feel a something under you,
As 'twere the claws of Death, which pull upon
The feet, resolved to have the head. Ah, Legg!
Some dragon fate has got its hold upon
Me. Dark days have their darker nights. To tell
The dreams that prey upon my mind and waste
My flesh, would turn thee into stone.
   L.   Dreams go
By contraries, the wise ones say, as sleep
And wakefulness are opposites. Myself
I have a thousand dreams ere aught in fact
Is like enough to be half cousin to
The last. Would we believe an oracle
When but each thousandth word had show of truth ?
   C. But when our dreams have full agreement with
Portentous signs, the double meaning must
Not have our slight. You know the night on which—
When evil powers had riot in the storm—
Through some malicious one, my lamp went out
And left a horrid darkness in the room.
That darkness had a meaning of its own—
A meaning supplemental to my dreams.
   L. The light and darkness were the whimsies of
A lamp, which is a mere insensate thing.
   C. Why was it in so meaningful a way ?
To answer that needs more than human wit.
There is a cause at back of all that is ;
And not a midge moves but there is a will

That moves it.   By so much the more—as it
Requires a greater power of intellect,
Which is the lever of a will—does the
Occult in nature ply responsive to
A will.   Tell me, what will can thwart our will
And means, producing darkness where was light,
But he who breeds dark things, as threatening us
With a malignant use of power? for things
Must match the mold that fashioned them.   In all
His works there is a unity in plan
And tendency of means.   Hence, when a lamp's
Extinguishment makes darkness, in a way
That challenges our wit, coincident
With darkness that confounds the senses of
Our friends, and both converging towards a point
Of ill,—a diabolic unity
Is manifest.   Ah, Legg!   It were enough
To stun a world to see a king reduced
To my extremity.   Be sure that ill
Is imminent; yea, violence against
My sacredly anointed majesty,
By this fanatical canaille, which has
No reverence for my royal sanctities,
Or yet the interests of the realm it rends.
Rebellion rank as that is raving mad;
Nor recks it what the power it topples o'er,
Rejoicing, rather, in the strength of wrath,
Which laughs to think what havoc it can make.
    L. But Cromwell, who is oracle to them,
Has some compunction and relenting ruth.
Admit, his motives may not be the best.
Yet odds it not what horse may bear you home,
Expectant of the meal he may not taste,
So you get safely there.
    C.   It staggers him
To see the part he played, and now to find

Himself in this predicament. But he
Has let his lion loose on us, and in
His helplessness he would undo the done,
Lest he himself should feel its hungry claws.
So blind is madness first, and then so weak.
Nature is such that, in a strait like his,
I would not risk a farthing on his aid,
Were he both soul and body of the whole,
Of which he is but the detested part—
The evil spirit dwelling in the whole.
No, Legg, the head of all must represent
Himself, nor recognize this traitor brood.
Behold these walls. For me they have a tongue.
Yea, every stone is eloquent, filling
The present with the past ; yet but to mock
My tender breast ; while these oppugnant and
Repugnant forces urge me to insure
My personal security as means present.
Their admonition shall not be in vain.

Enter Duke of GLOSTER, *attended.*

Gloster. Good-morning, father. Have those men been
    cross
To you ? They looked at me so like a dog
That wants to bite, I almost trembled ere
I passed the door.
    C.   Ah, son ! the morning is
But ill to me, and may to thee bring worse.
    G. How strange to have them treat a prince like that.
    C. And stranger still that so they treat a king.
    G. Why not command them to the tower ?
    C.   Poor child !
I wish I were as innocent as thou
In thy obtuse simplicity.
    G.   They tell
Me greater men have gone for less affront.

C. Since then the world is turning upside down.

G. Then what may happen to us if it does?

C. I mean, that wicked men have fought against
Thy father, and he is a prisoner here,
Where years ago he spent his happiest days ;
And he, instead of sitting on his throne
As king, may find the tower, and—and I know
Not what.

G.   Why so?

C.   Nay, they could hardly tell.

G. Suppose I go to them and ask them why?

C. They would not answer thee befittingly.
They would insult an angel—which thou art.   [*Aside.*

G. But you are always good ; so good ! If they
But knew it as I know they all would love
You as I love.

C.   Thy prattle ought to set
Mankind a-blush, to see their guile beside
Thy guilelessness. I know not but we grow
In folly as we grow in years. Know thou,
Poor child, that they may kill thy father.

G.   Kill
Their king ? my father ? one so good as you ?
Oh, where is God to let them do so ill ?
If I were God they all should find the tower.

C. Ay, ay, my child ! The world is full of ifs,
On which we blindly strike our tender shins.
Note well what now I say. When I am gone,
Thy brother Charles, by right, will be the king.
But they will hate him as they hated me,
And want to king thee in thy brother's stead.
But, as thou lovest me, consent thou not.

G. I will be torn to pieces first. I hate
The thought of them for hating you, and will
Forever hate what pleases them.

C.   Go then,

And keep thy father well in mind. Forget
Not all the precepts he has given. Be firm
In character, and shew thy royal blood;   .
So shall thy father live again in thee.
Oh, may thy years be as the golden calm
When evening burns her incense in the west.

  G. Why go? I fain would stay.

  C.   Go now, and come
Again. Make all thou canst of liberty. [*Exit Gloster.*
The tenderest ties are hardest to be broke. [*Weeping.*
Oh ! what more kingly than to be a man ?
And what more manly than to shed a tear
That comes from the divinest depth of soul ?

  L. At entrance of the duke, your Majesty
Was at the threshold of a subject in
Our thoughts—Ashburnham, Berkeley, and myself.
We have matured a plan for your escape ;
And we can serve you when the twilight glooms.

  C. To-night ?

  L.   To-night, while all our hearts are hot.
From purgatory into paradise.
The step comes none too soon.

  C.   Your tidings come
As 'twere a fortune to a pauper's home.
As good, I hope, will be results. You have
A plan, you say ?

  L.   A plan contingent on
Your Majesty's consent.

  C.   Consent indeed !
Ask my consent to keep my crown. What need
You next ?

  L.   When twilight deepens into dusk,
I will contrive to be upon the lawn
And wave my handkerchief three times to shew
That three white doves expand their wings to bear
You hence. The whither to, your Majesty

Will choose when on the way.

    C.   Well thought ; and may
It be well wrought !   But, lest our all depend
Upon a gossamer, we must consult
One skilled in more than earthly lore, and have
Him scan the aspect of the stars, thence to
Divine what indices they give.

    L.   We have
A woman with a will to do our will.

    C. Haste her to William Lilly, master of
The occult art, with this to speed his wit.

                                [*Counting some gold.*
And may she bring an answer to our mind !

                          [*Legg writes a note.   Then exit.*
Were I in London, these presumptuous rogues
Were as a shoal of shrimps before my net.
But what a gulf—those dozen miles—to span !
Though once it was right jocund exercise.
To leave the kingdom were an easier task,
Provided we can find a trusty ship :
So were they in the lurch, afraid to move,
While I were free to play my game at will.

                  Re-enter LEGG.

    L. She is dispatched, and I have signaled for
Dispatch to-night.

    C.   Then you anticipate ˙
The answer, making so my gold a gift.

    L. Good heaven forbid ! but in my mind has bee
The livelong day, the iteration of
A word, repeated as it were the tick,
Tick, ticking of a clock—to-night, to-night,
To-night.   It came not as a servant, but
As master of the will.   Nor wholly in
My sleeping or my wakeful hours ; but at
The birth-hour of the day the unseen power

Had wound my spirit up ; and it has kept
It's tick, tick, ticking in me ever since.
And, verily, I think it worth our heed.
For who, or what, should guide our mental gear,
In these involuntary grooves, but He
Who made it? Then, methinks, 'tis well we should
Have ears to hear, as said the priest this morn.

    C. Then what instructions ask you for the gold ?

    L. To tell what hour will guarantee success
To our emprise.

        C.   God grant he read aright !
Then may each rebel scratch his head till bald,
And stare his fellow blind.

      L.   A righteous prayer,
Deserving two amens. To whither would
Your Majesty escape ?

      C.   To France, were time
And circumstance in trim. But they, I fear,
Have need to lie in dry-dock for repairs,
Compelling us to take some jolly-boat
Of Fortune, and strike out for nearest land.

    L. The Isle of Wight would give meet shelter till
A ship were found.

      C.   Its governor dyed his hands
In loyal blood.

      L.   Yet not ferociously,
As one whose heart was flaming hot with ire,
But one whose easy indolence succumbed
To importunity. Some of your friends
Are his ; the thought of whom may come between,
As comes love's tender gift to motherhood
'Twixt man and wife. The august majesty
Of royalty withal would turn the scale,
Already half inclined, to honor's side.
Moreover, all are subtly bound in heart.
Hence those who hate us absent, seeing us,

May love ; since, in our absence, Fancy makes
Her moods the proxies for ourselves, until
Our presence disenchants her eye, when lo!
Our enemy becomes idolator.
But there the woman comes.

    C.   Would that all else
Might move with like alacrity. Bid her
    Come in. [*Exit Legg. Returns with the woman.*
[*To woman.*] Thou hast been nimble as a hare.

    W. They need have nimbleness who serve the king.

    C. Thy word deserves the favor of a king.
What message hast thou that may serve thy king?

    W. I wish your Majesty had seen his face,
The instant he began to trace his chart.
The sight was better than a shilling show.
It seemed as though the very stars were in
His eyes, and in his smile the twinkle of
Their light. I watched his finger trace from north
To south, and east to west—as though the heavens
Were but a spelling-book. And there he found
The heavenly houses, and consulted with
The lords, and every consultation made
His visage brighter still.

    C.   But prythee, tell
Us what he said.

    W.   'Twas wonderful to be
So near to heaven. It made me tingle to
My finger-ends.

    C.   What message did he send?

    W. Oh yes! He sent it by a word-of-mouth,
That none might pick one's pocket by the way.

    C. What said he then?

    W.   That all the signs agree
On six o'clock. Naught undertaken then
Can fail ; since 'tis the turning point between
The moons. But it must be exactly six,

Before the balance 'twixt the hours be lost.

C. Good service earns good pay. Here is a pound.

[*Exit Woman.*

She gave a curtsey worthy of a queen.

S. Note the coincidence. The something in
My mind kept telling me, to-night ; and now
These heavenly indices point out the hour.
That were enough to satisfy a Turk ;
Much more a Christian king.

C. Did she not say,
Exactly six ?

L. Exactly six.

C. What time
Have you ?

L. Quarter past one, within a tick
Or two.

C. I am just twenty minutes past.
With such discrepancy what data have
We to decide when is exactly six ?

L. Your Majesty has personal precedence,
Which carries with it right of time ; and this
Especially since you are first concerned.

C. Alas ! This life is all uncertainty.
And kings, with greatness, have the greater cares.
It seems me, I shall strike a line between
Your time and mine, and so again maintain
A balance twixt extremes. Meanwhile, I have
To write some letters. Then adieu to here.
Then what will follow that adieu ? Alas !
Time tells no secrets even to a king ;
Though favored ones may filch a hint or two.
Another week will shuffle all my cards.

[*Exeunt.*

ACT II.

Scene I. *The army at Corkbush field.*

Birch [*On a barrel*]. Soldiers ! Englishmen ! Saints !
    Remind ye all,
That better blood than that within your veins
Is not on earth. Titles and monkeyish
Deceits there are, by which a lazy few
Have found excuse for feeding on our sweat
And blood. But say ye all, and once for all :
Shall we be dogs, and they our fleas ?
    Shouts.   No, no !
    B. I knew your English blood would not consent.
Yet English hands have earned the bread they eat.
Feed them no more and they must earn their own.
The Maker of us all made men of all.
Hence all must have the common rights of men ;
And they, but men, must have no more than men.
Then, since the rich have more than is their right,
Of what is more 'tis right they should be shorn.
As men, then, let us ask and take our rights.
I ask a question. Give your hearts free play,
And let their answer leap from burning lips :
Shall we, who made, and now have saved, the land
Be churls, while they, who only squander what
We get, are gentlemen ; while yet with them
Ourselves have equal English blood ?
    Shouts.   No, no !
    B. Then shew ye are not slaves. Maintain your
        rights ;
For if ye slight your rights, your rights will slight
You in revenge. Away with kings, and all
The vermin swarming round the throne ! The saints
Are kings to God. Trust not to parliament.
We are the parliament of parliament,

And higher king or parliament is not.
As kings, then, let us rule ; as parliament,
Deprive ungodliness of what it has   .
Usurped.

    Shouts.   We will, we will !

    B.   What physic have
We that can cure a sick and bastard king ?

    Shouts. An axe !

    B.   Ye speak as prophets of the Lord.
But who shall be the doctor ?

    Shouts.   We.   The saints.

    B. Ay, ay ! For some who once were brave of speech
Are flunking now.

    A Voice.   Who ?

    B.   Who is that who sees
Not what a blind man ought to see ? Who had
The king in hand and let him go ? Who knew
And told the parliament when he escaped ?
Who, ever since, has had a soft word for
The runaway ? Don't dead leaves, dropping, shew
Which way the wind blows ? Who ? you ask. Ask
      him
Who feared some harm might hap the king. Ask him
Who calls him now, his Majesty. Ask him
Who fed him like a fighting cock. Ask him
Who prayed so much with us, while yet he brooked
The royal mummeries. Ask him ; for he
Can tell you all you wish to know ; and what
'Twere better none had never known. This makes
Our duty plain. When friends forsake we must
Befriend ourselves.

    Shouts.   Fairfax comes ! The general !

    B. What trumpery of the tongue ! A *general !*
A soldier gentlemen ! A mighty lord !
I call him Tom—plain, good old-fashioned Tom—
A name full good enough for any man.

                       [*Cheers in the distance.*

Who cheers is knave in heart or fool in mouth.
Look to the papers in your hats, " England,
With liberty, and soldiers' rights." That ought
To make your hearts thump like a drum.
 First Voice.   England
Hurrah !
 Second V. And liberty.
 Third V.   And soldiers' rights.
 B. [*Stepping down*]. Stand by your rights though
   death and hell say nay.
 A Voice. Fairfax is death and Cromwell hell.
     [*Fairfax approaches to address them.*
 Second Voice.   Hearken
To what he has to say.
 First V.   Hush ! Death would prate. [*Laughter.*
 Fairfax. Soldiers and fellow Englishmen, attend !
Our country is a tree, whose fruit sustains
Us all. Strike ye the trunk, ye strike the life
Of all ; but dig and dung about it, fruit
Will be for all. Now is the springtime, when
It needs your care ; and as you give that the
Return will be. Then count as yours who are
Old England's friends, and those her friends who are
The friends of all. " England, with liberty,
And soldiers' rights," I see is in your hats.
With England and your liberty you have
Your rights ; which rights your own right arms have won.
Then put those gauds away, and deeper write
Old England on your hearts ; so deeply, that
Your loyal deeds will prove 'tis there.
 Shouts.   Ha, ha !
Collar ourselves and give the rich the chain.
Granny, go home ! The leeches want our blood.
Open our mouth and shut our eyes and gulp
Whate'er you send us. Not so mouthy quite.
Oh, tweedle-dum-dee ! and cannot we see ?

F. I call on you, as Englishmen, to strip
Those papers from your hats.
   Shouts.   Bring you the king
To take them out. Away with king and lords !
   Cromwell. Take out those, I command, at once.
   B.   Come take
Them out who can.
   C. [*To a company of soldiers*]. Come on to loyal
     work.
Come on, brave lads.
            [*They follow him on the double quick.*
   A Voice.   Now lads ! now lads.
   C.   Seize ye
That prating knave. Take these two rogues. And this.
Take ye those three.
   A Voice.   Will no one help ?
   C.   Take him.
   A Voice. Where's Birch ?
   Another.   Making provision for his
     health.
   C. Those two. Out with your papers, all ; at once,
Or off you go. [*They obey.*] 'Tis well ye all obey.
[*Fourteen are taken to headquarters ; whom C. addresses.*
What think ye of yourselves, that ye who gave
Your names, your arms, your honors, to defend
The laws, are tramplers on the laws ? to save
The realm, are rebels 'gainst the realm ? to check
A lawless king, would make yourselves worse kings,
And leave us not the tatters of a law ?
Think ye we want a thousand kings, when we
Are sick of one ? a thousand kings, who know
No more of kingcraft than a bulldog of
The moon ? a thousand kings, bred to the axe,
The saw, the spade, turning your soldier caps
To crowns ? Think ye we want such kings to rule,
Who know so little how to rule themselves,

That ye stick up yourselves to mock us to
The teeth, in this defiant way ? Know ye,
Your lives are forfeit to the laws ye have
Defied. Ye ask the trial of the king
For trampling on the laws. Ye then, who want
To king it in the self-same way, shall try
The sauce ye recommend, by being tried
For this your breakage of the laws. So now
Prepare yourselves for what ye think the king
Deserves. Now, generals, to the work in hand.

> [*A few moments in conference ; then Fairfax
> addresses the prisoners.*

F. Soldiers ! It saddens me to think that ye,
Who earned so well your country's praise, should die
At last her enemies. Your crime is such
A greater cannot be. Ye set the laws
At nought, defy your officers, and turn
The army to a rabble. Know ye then,
That ye are rebels in the hands of law,
Whose eager lead would hasten on your doom.
What say ye? [*A pause.*] Nothing? Then ye own
       that there
Is nothing to be said ; and that is true.
Justice and Death are twins, so like we know
Them not apart. And Justice as a left
Hand holds, while Death as right hand smites. Then
       deem
Yourselves as dead. Yet Death himself, when he
Has wrenched the hapless body with his ills,
Full oft relents and gives it back to health
And joyance for a time. So we restore
You all, save three, from what ye all have earned ;
Which three we now select.   [*Cromwell selects them.*
    C.   Stand out.
    F.   Now go,
The rest of you, and deem your lives a gift ;

For which ye are indebted to our ruth.
But know ye, Justice will not spare again.
Ye three will now cast lots which one shall die.
                    [*Dice are brought and lots cast.*
Ye go as dead men snatched again to life.   [*To the two.*
Go shew ye know life's worth by living as
Ye ought.   [*They return.*]   This one **will** now be shot;
    and let
The rest take heed who do not wish like fate.
                    [*The man is shot.   Exeunt.*

SCENE II.   *Parliamentary* Generals *in council at Wind-
    sor, in a room of the castle.*

Fairfax. I leave it with you whether we have reached
The outpost of our duty to the realm;
And whether we can longer poise upon
A needle's point, in inactivity,
And free from fault.   I hold, our present deeds
Must vindicate our past.   The king must be
Condemned, or we.   He had his foot upon
The country's neck.   We threw him down, and have
Our foot on his.   Shall we allow his foot
The place it had ?   That is the question we
Must soon decide, or it will scout us and
Decide itself.   The king's heart, like a tree's,
Decays with age.   He is as paltering as
A Jew, as treacherous as a bog, and as
Malignant as a fiend.   Nor seems there ground
To hope for his amend.   We locked the door
Of power against him, and we hold the key.
So we declared our duty to the realm.
Shall we retract and say that we were wrong ?
That, or we must pursue the path we chose.
I hold, that what is done is right.   Hence right
It is to make assured it shall not be

Undone.   Ourselves withal are debtors to
Ourselves.   We counted not the value of
Our lives, but laid them at the country's feet ;
And many veins have drained their dearest drops.
We owe ourselves the fruits of so much cost.
Speak then your minds, as Englishmen ;
Then let us act as Duty gives the word.

   Cromwell. The realm is servant to the King of kings,
Who set the king a servant to the realm,
Which, hence, has right to call him to account.
She found him false to her and bade him pause.
His contumacy called out patience that
Had put a Job to blush.   She cited him
To meet her at the bar of battle, where
He was condemned.   She hoped his glacial heart
Might melt, and irrigate the land he froze.
His obduracy proves the match of hell.
We drop our cates as in a dead man's mouth.
For my part, I have aimed at duty's mark,
Trying to serve the realm through him the king.
In that I stopped at nothing short of life,
To make him sensible of duty's claims,
And end the stupor of his lethargy,
In hope he might arouse, admonished by
Experience, to fulfill his trust.   So far
I went, so much I sacrificed, that men
Suspect in me duplicity and deep
Collusion ; yea, complicity in guilt.
This price I paid, to find my service as
A drop of water swallowed by the sea.
His heart is as the fate of Lucifer.
Now, as our cause was just, and is, while he
Remains incurable, I turn and say
To Mercy :   Hide thou thy insulted face ;
To Justice :   Do the utmost of thy will.
Henceforth I serve the realm without the king.

Ireton. We want no wary crocodile to weep
With open jaws; no eel whose tongue is deft
In tricks of speech, while yet so slippery that
The firmest grasp of faith is holding on
To nothing in the end. Methinks our men,
Untangled by the webs of sophistry,
And one in suppliance at a throne of grace,
Are in a purer air than we, with sight
To see beyond. Their courage ought to make
Us blush, as blush I do to think of it.
And as the more I think, the more I blush—
Ay, till the blood is mad-hot in my veins—
That we, who are the masters of the king,
Should pause before the memory of his power.
Think of our servant faithless to his trust.
Think of him having eaten, drank, and worn
Our best, then turned and paid us with his fist,
And ask : Shall our endurance have no end ?
Think of the realm that gave its destinies
In trust to us, then ask again : Have we
Fulfilled that trust, while still we parley with
The cause of all her woes? We must be right
Or wrong. If right, go on. If wrong, retrace
Our steps. But right we are as God above
Is right. Then let us vindicate the right.

C. He who jilts Mercy, Justice takes in hand.
Here, then, to Justice relegate the king,
By executing law without a wince.
To that his conduct challenges ; and I
Am ready to accept the gage. The laws !
The laws ! The people and the laws must meet
Him foot to foot and have it out. Here then,
In England's name, I take the gage. Ay, in
The triple kingdom's name I take it up.

[*A knock.*

Who comes?

Enter Sir JOHN BERKELEY.   CROMWELL *sits down.*

F. What want you here?

B.   His Majesty
Sends letters to the generals.   [*Handing them to Fair-
     fax.*]   Here is one
From Colonel Hammond.

F.   To the generals !   Well,
Withdraw yourself and wait you at our call.   [*Exit B.*

I. Another wriggle of the eel, to slip
Our grasp.

C.   These letters are the climax of
His craft, to drive a wedge between ourselves
And parliament, by having us ignore,
And so renounce it as our master,—which
It is,—and, by our treating with himself,
To place him in its stead.   While thus his left
Is offered us, his right hand he extends
For Scottish lips to kiss.   So, with the two,
He would confound the parliament and serve
Himself ; in which he would confound us all.
Confounded be his treachery !   Contempt
Were an unmerited civility,
And silence more than his desert.   Yet speech
Were vainly cast on the Sahara-waste
Of his malign stupidity.   Then let
Us give the best rebuff we may, to make
Him sensible that we are sensible
Of his designs.

I.   In gambler slang he talks
About his *game*, in which, as gambler, he
Would cheat.   Only an honest wariness
Can foil his craft.   I sanction what is said
About rebuffing him.

Lambert.   Let Naseby put
An echo in his ear until he reels.
Remind him that the masters of to-day

Are not named Charles. Belike, he has forgot.

Harrison. Think not his craft exhausts itself on us.
It is an eye which looks all ways at once.
These letters are a segment of a scheme
Whose broad periphery holds unnumbered spokes.
For while he aims to disunite his foes,
He is intriguing with the riff-raff of
The world to let it loose upon them. Hence
We need—defense, a pound ; offense, a ton.

   F. Call in Sir John. [*Enter Berkeley.*] Inform your
     master that
We have no jurisdiction ; hence no right,
Nor yet the wish, to treat with him. We serve
The parliament, to which his letters shall
Be sent, with Colonel Hammond's, which, no doubt,
Is incidental to the king's.

        [*Exit B. Cromwell and Ireton frowning.*
   C.   Well rid !
And better if we never see him more.   [*Exeunt.*

SCENE III. *Midnight. In a close.* Sir JOHN BERKE-
   LEY, *talking in low tones with a* General.

   General. The interests of the king are urging him
To flee ; for Carisbrook weaves his shroud, since o'er
Against his name the skull-and-crossbones of
A fatal purpose has been traced.
   Berkeley.   Have all
The generals part and lot in this ?
   G.   You saw
The vulture frown that on their craggy brows
Perched, ready for a swoop of wrath upon
You, as your errand slipped your tongue. Then were
Their feelings under hard restraint, else had
You found their talons in your heart. There is
An epidemic of distrust, which rates

The king's word less than one per cent. its face.
Hence can I pledge, not one would disapprove
Appeal to law's arbitrament, or blink
To see the axe.   Let his persistence break
The bands of their restraint—look out for blood ;
And that more sovereign than has yet been shed.

    B. Such deed was never in a Christian land ;
And Heaven forbid that England see it first.
Indeed, it is too monstrous to be done.
The soul of Horror shudders at the thought.
The very heavens would shut their shining eyes
And weep ; while earth's great rocky heart would break.
Should men once come to that, this world would scarce
Be worth the living in.

    G.   His Majesty
Is bringing them to that.   He had his friends,
With Cromwell at their head, till friendship smacked
Of treason to the realm.   A flood-tide in
Events there is ; and he who breasts it sinks.
The adjutators, with the army at
Their back, o'erwhelm the generals until, now,
Not one resists.

    B.   Can I hold interview
With Cromwell ?

    G.   Ask to place a musket at
His breast.   The cats'-eyes of Suspicion watch
His leanings towards the king, whom he would serve
Within the limits of the ancient law.
The king would not be served, demanding that
For which we took the gage, as though 'twere his
To give us terms, and ours to take them with
A Thank-your-Majesty.   For one, I hope
The king will flee the storm while flight may be,
And, in the calm of mental solitude,
Perceive the posture of affairs, relax
His haughtiness, and be content to take

The possible.   This chance despised, or foot
Of tardiness in taking it—farewell
To crown, to England ; ay, to more than that !
    B. Letters I have for Cromwell from the king.
    G. They may not be delivered by yourself ;
Nor would I take the service on myself ;
For none is suffered to communicate
With you on penalty of death : withal,
The labor were not worth a paltry groat.   [*Exeunt.*

SCENE IV.   CHARLES *at Carisbrook, sitting alone.*

Berkeley [*Entering*].   I am amazed to find your Ma-
                    jesty
Still here ; whom I supposed some days ago
In France, where Danger could not touch you with
A finger-tip ; while here it holds you in
Its arms, which tighten every hour.
    Charles.   Your nerves
Have lost the equability that lets
The soul lie calm as water-lilies on
A lake.   For my part, I have felt so long
My interest flapping in the wavelets, that
The very motion causes drowsiness.
    B. Alas, it is a deadly drowsiness !   [*Aside.*
    C. Meanwhile, the roots may thrive no whit the less.
At all events, I am content to wait
Till Fortune whispers further in my ear.
    B. Wait, while the teeth of Danger graze your skin !
Wait, while black Doom is laughing at your hopes !
This island is a dungeon, lacking but
A turnkey at the door ; a lack that will
Not be delayed.
    C.   You see the surface of
Affairs.   I feel a ground swell, whose deep force,
Unseen, is making for deliverance.

B. What means your Majesty ?

C.   The English are
But a divided house, each half of which
Will help the other half to fall.   The Scots
Can make it tumble either way.

    B.   The Scots !
(Pardon me if my zeal outruns my reverence.)
A ship had served you better than the Scots ;
Not wrenching conscience, while it did your will.
The Scots reck not a paltry groat what comes
Of you, so they be served.   To trust them is
To cast your anchor on a drifting floe.

    C. They cannot bind my conscience with my tongue,
And fetter me in slavery with a word.
To-day is free to meet to-day's demands.
To-morrow must be free as is to-day.
What serves me now is the demand of now.
What serves me hence will be my duty hence ;
For I must do the best when best it is.
Of course, their service is to serve themselves.
. But if they round it and we catch the game,
We need not ask their motive for the chase.
Moreover, this desire to serve themselves
Will make them care for me, through whom must come
The serving of themselves.

    B.   To use you as
A shoe, then cast you out.

    C.   Where, think you, will
My eyes be then ?

    B.   Where are they now ? is far
More pertinent ; and where the parliament's,
With such a nudge as you have given its wrath ?
Be sure, 'tis neither sleeping nor in mood
To wait the motions of the Scots.   Belike,
My letter missed you, or your hopes would turn
No eye to England.

C.   Oh !—the generals of
An army shattered with its mutinies,
Resolve to hurl the incohesive mass
At parliament, the country, Scots, Irish,
King, world, God, everything! Yes, I remind
Me of the threatened feat ; I do.

B.   I can
Assure your Majesty that Windsor has
A key on Carisbrook that can lock you up
As safely as a bottled flea. Why, scarce
A step you take but what it knows the length ;
Or word escapes your lips and passes by
Its ear, save as that word is double-locked
With privacy. Nay, I were loth to swear
It could not inventory half the thoughts
That, for a week, have struggled in your mind.
Thus does it have you in its eye ; yea, in
The middle of its palm. Then think you it
Will stand, in blank stolidity, and see
The Scots convey you thence ! But are
The Scots more trusty than the parliament ?
If 'tis your *cause* they wish to serve, your flesh
And bones are not essential as the means.
If *you* they want, mistrust some barter should
It serve their ends. Remember Newcastle ;
As well you may.   [*A pause.*

C.   And has a Stuart come
To be a thing—a piece of merchandise
For men to haggle o'er, like hungry Jews?

B. They who have found a market value in
A king, are tigers that have tasted blood.
Remember Newcastle, I say ; which has
A mouth to drop a word in Carisbrook's ear.
Belike, your Majesty will not be deaf.

C. This morn it pleased me, when I set the dogs
Contending for a bone, to think how great

Contention I have caused. I realize
To-night how hard it is to be the bone.
You talk escape. Know then, my word is given
To stay, and pledged my honor with my word.

B. How pledged your honor saving with a word?
The word then, not your honor, is at stake ;
And words are windy things, which fill the sails
Of our designs and waft us as we steer.

C. O Berkeley ! It is time I gather up
The fragments of my dignity and shew
The majesty of kinghood, when they bring
Me thus to bay. I feel a royal glow
Of indignation, urging me to fling
Defiance in their teeth and laugh to scorn
Their impotence. I do defy them. I
Defy the dirty rogues to smut me more ;
Defy them to withhold from me the realm.
The bird will find its nest, and I my throne.
'Tis here, with courage citadeled in faith,
I take my stand.

B.   Prudence gives Courage eyes ;
And here you need them. Were you once in France,
Your friends would feel that you were free to act ;
Your foes be foiled, and stand in sheer amaze ;
And soon the country would demand its king.

C. The past has much inscribed on memory's walls
That tells of failure, till I weary of
Escape that ever puts me farther from
The throne.

B.   The problem is, the farthering of
You from the block.

C.   What, execute a king !
Their lawful king ! Nay, Berkeley, never that !
Not while a drop of England's blood remains.
The instinct of the beggar on the street,
Up to the duke beneath his coronet,

Would stir revulsion in their startled souls,
Mad they may be, as common madness goes ;
But madness cannot be so mad as that.

 B. Call it their madness, or whate'er we may ;
It is a madness with a steady nerve ;
A madness born like thunder 'mid the clouds
Of threatening visages, which tell of strength
Behind. There is no incoherence in
The madness of their speech, but logic—a
Relentless syllogism of resolve,
Which leaves the one conclusion on their lip.

 C. It cannot be.

 B.   Heaven save you from the proof !

 C. Ah, Berkeley ! I have plumbed our nature to
Its depth and found a slimy bottom to
It all. Think what we may, the world is ruled
By craft ; and ever most when cornered in
Some strait extremity. This life is war,
Where sword must measure lengths with sword, and
   lance
With lance. Craft, with an honest motive at
Its back, is goodness good enough to serve
A saint. Not that, however, have these knaves,
Who court the parliament and fear the king.
Their craft is knavish, for a knavish end,
And must be worsted with an honest kind.

 B. What kind of craft will blunt an axe's edge ?

 C. Tut, tut ! Thou hast the dregs of nightmare in
Thy pate. I warrant thee, their goblin hints
Come from the gruesome graveyard of their fears.
Hence why they sheet themselves to play the ghost,
Thinking to shock my reason with the cheat,
To make my knees forget their wonted strength,
And, while I shake, to steal my royalty.
Beshrew me, if I fail to blast their hopes !

 A knock. *Enter* Colonel HAMMOND *with* guard.

H. Orders received command the servants of
Your Majesty to leave the isle to-night.
A boat is waiting to convey them hence.

    C. Waiting?

    H.   Yes, waiting at the pier to slip
Her cable and away.

    C.   What means it? and
With such a shock of haste?

    H.   The order first,
And then your Majesty shall be informed.

    C. Who orders it?

    H.   Those whom I serve.

    C.   There is
Unseemliness in such abrupt commands.

    H. My ear belongs to Duty, not Debate.   [*A pause.*

    C. So, Berkeley, we must part.   O trusty friend!
I know not what can compensate me for
Thy loss. Thou wert the last star peeping through
The clouds, which now close over thee. Who knows
What fury may be in the heart of this
Dark storm before we meet again?

    B.   I fear
Me we shall never meet.   [*Weeping.*

    C.   Nay, do not spring
My heart aleak, and sink me in the sea
Of my distress.

    B.   Heaven grant these tears, which come
Too soon, may be my last for you.   Better
They were my blood if that had better served.

    C. Take heart.   We need but justice on our side
To come out right at last.   Sure as I am
The Lord's anointed, so I have the seal
Of His assurance that my cause is just.
Which cause is His.   Hence He is on my side,
Implying that my foes are butting at
Omnipotence.   Seek harbor where thou canst;

And when the gale is past, come thou and share
The favor of thy king.
  B.   Heaven only knows
What buffetings may come between. .
  C.   Perhaps.
But there is boundless sea-room for perhaps.
Perhaps our vision is at fault. God grant
It may be so. But hap what may, God and
Mine own integrity remain ; in which
I have a kingdom for the soul, beyond
The permutations of the outward life.
  H. Excuse me if I ask your haste. [*To Berkeley.*]
   But I
Am in the stress of duty's urgency.
  C. Farewell ! I never knew the meaning of
The word before.
  B.   'Twas never half so sad
Before. It seems a prophecy of ill. [*Exit with guards.*
  C. Explain the why of this atrocious haste.
  H. The powers that be are cognizant of those
The Scots, whose machinations compass your
Removal hence, and thus are thwarting them.
  C. The doings of the generals, I suppose,
To plume their popinjay authority.
  H. The generals, having tortured long their wits
To tie the severed threads of amity
For those whose hands are red with kindred blood,
Abhor the thought of staining them anew.
Of this I know full well ; for one of them
Has torn concealment from his heart and shewn
Me what was not for every eye.
  C.   So would
He have compunction shrive his evil deeds,
While he compounds with Justice, to elude
The grasp of Retribution. Pious dupe !
Repentance wrung from us with Death's gripe on

Our throat, would vainly cheat the evil one.
Too well the Devil knows his own for that
Device to blind his eyes and rob him of
His dues.

    II.   ' Cromwell has been your friend.   To serve
You, he adventured nigh beyond his death ;
So nigh, another step had swept him off
His feet, and sooner swamped your Majesty.

    C. Oh, prudent man !   Like truant schoolboy, he
Has wantoned in the shallows, where the splash
Of war made merriment ; but feeling now
The onrush of the tide whose flood is towards
The throne, he seeks a safer standing-place.
Such prudence has a palpitating heart,
Yet proves politic prescience on his part.
So all of them are in a quandary.
The sport is ended, and they need a king.
But, having labored to eviscerate
My royalty, and leave no more than a
Mere mummy of prerogative, they want
With that to simulate a king.   For dread
They do to meet a living king.   But they
Have failed.   Nor can they aught without my free
Consent.   They still will find me king, without
Whom they can have no law, no order, nor
A thread to hold the realm together ; but
Stark Anarchy will stride with bloody feet,
And hurl the bolts of havoc at the land,
Till Chaos monuments their madness o'er
Its grave.

    II.   I wish your Majesty a right
Interpretation of events,and a
Due homage to necessity.   But sure
It is that, hitherto, your policy
Has put the realm in an oppugnant mood,
Which only change of policy can change.

Unwise it is, unhorsed, to flaunt a red
Flag in the country's face.

C.   Kings have kings' thoughts
And ways.

H.   And others other thoughts and ways ;
And when they clash the weakest finds the wall.
But Duty calls me hence. Wise thoughts be with
Your Majesty.   [*Exit.*

C.   Fools deem their betters fools,
And hence are prodigal of their advice,
Which only fools will take. The weakest, says
He, thinking multiples are strength ; whereas,
Omnipotence, while everything, is but
The unit next to naught. The weakest? No !
I represent this One—Omnipotence.
And woe to those who find the day of wrath !   [*Exit.*

Scene V. *Kingston-on-Thames. Hall of the Castle.*

  Duke of Buckingham. What pigmies prank them-
    selves in giant's mail !
Hodge aping royalty with buckram strut !
To see their madness foaming at the mouth
Is fit to make an Etna of one's heart ;
Ay, and to send the red-hot lava through
The veins. Our king—our God-anointed king—
Is held by their unhallowed hands in dire
Duress ; while doom hangs, by a single hair,
Above the heads of our nobility.
The past foreshadows what is still in store.
War it has been these years, with blare and blood—
Stark force in carnival upon the grave
Of all that made old England once so proud.
And war 'twill be so long as these wild beasts
Are rampant, till the country's bones are bare.
O good my lord ! it maddens me till I

Could wish a thousand skulls were one, and I
Might cleave that one and rid the land of this
Infection.

  Earl of Holland. Zeal, not madness, save as it
May be mad zeal, which dares the Devil to
His teeth, is what the day demands. Great deeds—
Heroic deeds, are Fortune's currency, in which
May be the ransom of the king ; and these
Are ours ; of which, I trust, we shall not give
A niggard's dole.

  B.   By the eternal stars !
I swear that Buckingham is ready to
Be spendthrift for.his king. My blood, my brain,
My heart, my very soul is his ; as well
Befits a true and loyal lord. Nil crown,
Ill coronet. Strike out the sun, then woe
Betides his satellites.

  II.   That minds me of
My dream but yesternight. Sleep left my lids,
Refusing to be wooed, when horrid thoughts,
For an attenuated hour, stole like
So many serpents through my mind and slimed
My senses o'er with chills. At length, I slept
And dreamt. The inky clouds were blotted o'er
The sky, and earth was glum as Winter in
The dumps ; while Nature was disconsolate
As disappointed Love. I wore my cheeks
To wrinkles with the runnels of my tears ;
For I was as the hue and humor of
The day. But suddenly the sun emerged,
In all-diffusive splendor, when my heart
Gave three hard thumps—the sign of luck—and I
Awoke, to find a messenger arrived
With tidings of uprisings for the king ;
On which, I felt most guilty that I lay
Supine, with glory's trumpet blaring in
My ears.

B.   That dream is prophecy, at back
Of which the tidings trumpet us to arms ;
And, by Jove's thunder, I shall not be deaf ;
Else, may that thunder strike me doubly dead !
But first the tidings in their amplitude.

H. Pembroke keeps Cromwell at his futile task.
At Maidstone, Fairfax came within an ace
Of round defeat ; and everywhere he finds
The country as a common thick with gorse,
Which tears his forces every step he takes.
Lord Goring has an army swooping down
On London ; while Capel and Lucas keep
The rebels tied to Colchester.   In fact,
The country is a warren, where the king's
Friends leap from every bush ; the like of which
Has not been seen before.   Yet here we are,
As idle as a pair of iron dogs.   [*Enter the Jester.*

B. Such tidings give more cheer than tuns of
      wine,
And call for pikes and muskets to the front.
What muster can we make of bone and thew ?
I ween the beck of Buckingham will bring
A thousand yeomen to the rendezvous,
With hearts as lusty as a king could ask.

H. And Holland's word is worth a thousand more.

Tommy, the Jester. My master's dish has need to grow
      to fill
So many mouths.

H.   Yes, Tommy ; but with mouths
To clean the dish are hands to fill again.

T. A thousand men a-making furmity !

H. No, doing glorious deeds by ridding us
Of rebels.

T.   How ?

H.   By killing them.

T.   I see,

And making rebel broth of them to fill
The dish.

H.   I fear the broth would poison us.

T. Beware then of the meat. But what will fill
The dish ?

H.   These men will save the king, and so
Save all of us.

T.   If they can save the king
And all of us, what need we of a king ?

H. Without a king, to wear the crown and have
Authority, the kingdoms have no head.

T. All this ado to get a man to wear
A crown and use authority ! Odds me !
But I could wear a crown, with fangles to
My toes, and, with enough authority,
Kick all of you to Scotland, and swell out
My head as big as fifty cabbage-heads.
So why not make me king ?

H.   Why, Tommy, kings
Are great and grand, living in palaces.

T. Give me the palaces and I will live
In them, then be as grand as you will pay
For, and as great as grouse and hares can make me.

H. But few, I ween, would care to make thee
  king.

T. The world is full of fools, who call me fool.
The difference 'twixt us is in this : I know
Myself a fool, and so am wise ; they take
Themselves for wise, and so are fools. They spit
The earth in face and call her lout, then cry
Like babies for the moon to play with, and
Grow dumpish when it baffles them. England
Spurns Tommy and boo-hoos for Charles, when, did
She know it, Tommy were the cheaper king.

H. Take care, or Tommy may be rebel, rank
As Cromwell, Fairfax and the rest, and black

As night with neither moon nor star.

T.   Small odds
'Twixt fools and rebels if the rebels all
Are fools. Small odds 'twixt day and night. The day
For deeds, and night for dreams. But whether deeds
Make dreams for night, or dreams make deeds for day,
Would take a greater fool than me to tell.
Belike, 'tis both ; for what we eat makes dreams,
And what we dream gets fashioned into deeds.

H. Now, Tommy, take thy riddle by the tail,
And turn it round that we may see its head.

T. Nay, good my lord ; when such like riddles leave
Our heads they are but tales, which wag as wagged
Our tongues.

H.   Then give us further tale about
The deeds and dreams.

T.   Your lordship's deeds dispose
Of beef and ale, which, by some alchemy
Within, are turned to dreams ; and then the dreams,
Digested in the maw of Fate, are turned
To deeds. Thus are your dreams of noble stuff,
Begetting kindred deeds ; while Tommy's, made
Of furmity, have Fool tattooed upon
The foreheads of them all.

B.   Would beef and ale
Breed wise dreams in a fool ?

T.   Last night they did.

B. Pray tell us how.

T.   Luck had a merry mood
And gave me beef and ale, which bred a dream
That were a credit to a king.

H.   Tell it,
And let us judge its quality. ·

T.   The day
Was sulking in a drizzle, with the night
At hand, and I was trudging on a jaunt :

When, right anent my nose, a pit yawned, not
Two feet across. For aught I knew, it was
A hole bored through the earth to let rogues drop
Into the nether pit. But, being more
A fool than rogue, I thought to clear it at
A jump. Stock-still, I scratched my pate, in hope
To find a grain of lucky wit ; when, as
I scratched, the hole grew full four feet. I spat
Upon my hands, and lo ! six feet it was
Across. My resolution got upon
Its mettle then, and I was on the bend,
When something grabbed me by the scruff and said,
" Beware, trust not the resolutions born
On rainy days ! " The hole was eight feet wide.
But, not to wed a coward to a fool,
I jumped. Alack ! Had I gone up instead
Of down the moon had found a fool. Then I
Awoke to hear a gurgle at the eaves.
Belike, your lordships hear it raining now.

    B. A fool's dream after all.

    T.   A wise dream by
A fool.

    H.   There, this diversion is enough. [*Exit Tommy.*

    B. Tommy has fool-wit for fool-dreams. But dreams,
Belike, are as their source. When noble minds,
In the soul's inner solitude, behold
Unbodied things, a noble quality
Is in their dreams ; and yours were worthy of
A king, as it was for a king, and sent
Withal conjunctive with events that give
It their attest. To action then. Our force
Is full two thousand, of the stanchest stuff
That England has to shew, with everything
To win, and everything to make them win.
That force is worth its quadruple of three
Short months ago ; as much of three to come.

Thus we awake at the alarum bell
Of Providence. The rebel strength, dispersed
In fragments, and engaged in futile siege,
Leaves us the freedom of the hurricane.
Once in the field, our besom soon will sweep
The litter of their forces from our path ;
Courage will nerve the country's heart, and we
Shall find our army growing as we march.

    II. Time is prime factor now. Days are as weeks,
Weeks months. When can we be arrayed, ready
To give the trumpet answer with our step ?

    B. One week and Buckingham will rendezvous.

    II. Agreed. One week and Kingston's cocks will
      crow
At tramp of Holland's men. Speed is our word.
God grant the word may find its match in deeds !

                              [*Exeunt.*

    SCENE VI. *A group of* rustics *opposite an inn at a
       country fair. A* singer *selling ballads.*

    Singer. Come, loyal hearts, and hear a loyal song.
    First Rustic. Pray, what is loyal nowadays ?
    S.   The song.
    First R. Sing. Loyalty, like measles, may be catch-
      ing.   [*He sings.*

      O green-clad isle ! O sea-washed isle !
        The fairest under heaven !
      We lose the light of thy dear smile,
        Because thy heart is riven.
      A dreadful dern has bowed thy head,
        As bows the bearded barley ;
      The rose-bloom red thy face has fled,
        In pining for thy Charley.

      Oh, Charley is a bonny name ;
        And bonny he who bears it ;

Ay, bonny is the country's fame
　　Whose throne so proudly wears it.
But woe's-a-me that Englishmen
　　Should be so blind and snarly,
They whip us when we ask again
　　For our own darling Charley!

By day, the wood-wind wails and sighs;
　　By night, the sad owl screeches;
The sea-wave drops its head and dies
　　In sobs along the beaches.
Then lend an ear to Pity's call;
　　No more let faction parley;
But, ere we all shall faint and fall,
　　Oh, give us back our Charley.

First R. Bah! black-sheep loyalty, which needs a
　　knife.

Second R. Heaven sour their porridge who have got
　　the king.

Third R. Trust them for eating porridge, sour or
　　sweet.

Second R. Heaven plague the traitor crew at any rate.

First R. Hell might prefer to undertake the task,
In honest wrath, to find them in its way.

Third R. Where stand'st thou on the question of the
　　king?

First R. About the middle; and it circles me
Without an end.

Third R.　　　　There needs a break in things
To make an end.

First R.　　　　A break might make two ends—
An end of Charley and of thee.

Third R.　　　　　　　　Things were
Not worse were doomsday here.

First R.　　　　　　　　That may be what
We need, to rake the dead kings from their dust,
And get them and the quick at loggerheads
While other folk have peace.

Third R.　　　　　　　　Nay, loggerheads

We have, but not the peace.

  First R.   One loggerhead
Against the realm.

  Fourth R. [*From behind*]. I hear a tongue that trips
It to a traitor's tune.

  First R. [*Turning*]. I hear a tongue
That serves an addled skull.

  Fourth R.   Takest thou me
To be a chicken-heart?

  First R.   Chicken or goose,
The heart is illy stirred that stirs thy tongue
To make so ill a prate.

  Second R.   God give us back
Our Charley.

  First R. He has better use for him,
And may have better still when reckoning comes.

  Third R. We want no mean-bred chaps, who need a
           dame
To keep their noses clean, to mountebank
As kings.

  First R. Cromwell, they say, has king's blood in
His veins. But he has acted as befits a king.
And he has been more kingly than the king;
While Charley played the mountebank,
And, by his clumsy vaultings, lost a throne.

  Second R. We need a head to keep the body safe.

  First R. Ill serves the head that cannot keep itself.
A cabbage-head were worth a dozen such.

  Fifth R. [*Just come up*]. Treason! treason! Here
        is a fellow talks
Against the king.

  First R.   And prythee who is king?
The fellow bottled up in Carisbrook, with
The thumb of Cromwell for a cork? No, no.
The king's king is the king for me.

  Fifth R.   Wait till

He gets his dues, and that will cork thy gab.

First R. Ay, when eternity is worn away.
This king of thine would king it o'er the soul.
The Devil has his wits, and England he
Would mortgage to the Devil, and ask Heaven
To ride us down to ruin.   But a power
There is across this Baalim's path, with sword
Of flame.   Let Carisbrook answer him who doubts.

    Fourth R. Thou ranting recusant! Some gibbet
      aches
To get thee in its arms; and get it will
Before the autumn wears its weeds: so sure
As all the signs in heaven and earth agree.
That blazing star fell not last night for nought;
Nor Maslin's cow brought forth a calf, pied with
A crown, for nought: nor is old London mad
To get her Charley back for nought; nor is
The pibroach piping up the Scots for nought.
I tell thee, some cross-road will have a spot
To shew thy dangling bones.

    Sixth R.   A sight to please
Thy king.

    Fourth R. Another traitor here!

    Sixth R.   Traitor
Is he who serves a traitor king; and he
A traitor king who breaks the laws.   Well dost
Thou threaten in his name.   But know thou, he
Who judges so shall so be judged, though king
He be; for there is One to whom a king
Is common clay, and in whose scales the crown
Is on the debit side.   But tell me, why
Art thou so whist about the Welch?   What sign
Was that when Cromwell bent them o'er his knee
And slapped obedience into them?   And what
When he shall make the Scots respect the rod?
Thy signs will need another gypsy then.

Fourth R. To-morrow's wind may not be measured by
To-day's.

First R. Thy wind will not when Charley gets
His dues.   .

Seventh R. My Jack was wee when first the strife
Began ; but now he works, a lusty lad.
Through all these years it has been kill and waste,
And waste and kill, till every family
Is dressed in black. O lads, it sickens me
To think of it ! For pity's sake, I think,
'Tis time to stop, for all the odds I see
It make to us ; except it be to cost
Us sore in blood and store.
                [*The village crier rings his bell.*
             What bruit is this

Mid-fair ?

Crier. Glory to God ! who wreathes afresh
Old England's brow. The Scots are beaten till
Their carcasses strew half of Lancashire.
Ten thousand prisoners are in Cromwell's hands,
Besides their stuff, too much to reckon up.
So evermore may God defend the right !

Shouts. Hurrah for England ! Hip, hip, hip, hurrah !

Fourth R. That's glorious news.

Second R.   The lousy Sandy's have
Their fill at last.

First R.   Now who is king ?

Fourth R.   England
Is king.

First R. England indeed ; not Charley's ghost.

Sixth R. With fifty lives he could not well as this.
He never did a deed that made us proud.
He never made a promise that he kept,
Except it were the Devil had his word.
Because we humbly asked him for our rights,
He slapped us with an army in the face :

And blood has flowed from that day unto this.

First R. He brought a madcap prince to harry us.
He held up England like a toothsome cate,
That foreigners might come and suck her strength.
He brought the Irish papists to our shores.
He stirred the Welch to strike us to the hilt.
He hired the Scots to rob and murder us.
And take himself, when shewing bravest grain,
It was in stabbing at his country's heart.
Nay, tell us what he has not that is mean,
Unkingly, damnable?   And now that he
Is caged, he roars in helpless wrath, to prove
That still he thirsts for English blood.   Long as
He lives he will but be a thorn to us.
Only by dying can he do us good.

Third R. Thou hast a mile and fifty thousand rods
Of gab.   Thy tongue is like a flail, and thou
Hast threshed the village till it aches.

Seventh R.   High time
It is we had an end.   At all events,
The lousy Scots have got their fill.

Sixth R.   It is
To answer, whether all these years of war
And woe shall count for nought, and gibbets, filled
With Englishmen, be hung by every road,
Because we love the English laws.   The Scots,
Whom thou despisest, are his hope who is
Thy hope, who brought this war and woe.   The Scot's
Blood in him leans that way.   But England's life
Is not in Charley's breath ; for she has flogged
Both him, Scot, Welch, and Irish, one by one,
Proving we need not such a nobody.
They who have got him are the greater king.

Second R. The topmost dog is often in the wrong.

Sixth R. But here we know the under dog is wrong ;
And certainly the upper dog is best.

Third R. Who made thy head so big to judge a king?

Sixth R. A little head may know that horsebeans are
Not gingerbread; that black is black; that black
And white are two; and that a king's lie is
A common lie. And this great king of thine
Is liar o'er and o'er; ay, fifty of
The common kind could be no worse. Think'st thou
His kinghood makes his sin less sin than ours,
To Him who sees all in their nakedness?
He who is most a man is most a king.

Fourth R. No telling what this Cromwell were if once
A king. They say he is a canting knave,
A mouthing hypocrite, who hates the church.
Then liefer would I trust a dog to keep
My dinner, or a lawyer with my purse,
Than such to keep my soul. His soldiers, too,
They say, have such a prate of holy things
As ill befits their quality. Suppose
Him king, and these rapscallions ranting in
The church, polluting with their bawdries what
Is not intended for our common touch.
It were enough to turn the moon to blood.

Sixth R. Thou lickspit! Thinkest thou thy fellow-
        man
Can keep thy soul, who cannot keep his own?
That amices, and stoles, and surplices,
And holy flunkeyisms, satisfy
The Maker of the soul? or that He spurns
An Englishman with honest speech upon
An honest lip? I would not screw my soul
Down to the point where it could think such thoughts.
Men buy not sanctity at draper's shops;
Nor get it from a bishop's finger-ends:
Bishop withal by grace of godless king.
But, as the dew, it filters from above,
On every heart that opens like a flower.

Know thou, that Cromwell, though far kinglier than
The king, is asking no one to be king.
Yet here, forsooth,—because he makes no odds
'Twixt children whose true mother's name was Eve,
But sweeps the path between their souls and God,—
Thou deemest him a knave.   Would God we had
More knavery of the kind !

    Seventh R.   Well, we have drubbed
The Scots, as they deserved.

    Sixth R.   Ay, ay.   And in
Our drubbing them we drubbed a Stuart Scot—
A Scot who is the Scottest of them all.   [*Exeunt.*

ACT III.

    SCENE I. *In a tent at Colchester ; near the camp.*

    Fairfax. What say you of the temper of the house?
    Ludlow. This parliament has not an honest heart.
Chicane and Treason, as the demons of
The hour, flap their black pinions over it,
With buzzard instinct led to carrion deeds.
It does not serve the kingdoms, but the king.
The realm may perish, but God save King Charles !
Its every breath is redolent of king.
Its real hopes revolve around the king.
Its true affections aureole the king.
Belike, its dreams are full of phantom kings.
Yet that is not its utmost of offense.
It compasses the means to bring him back.
Still, 'tis not merely lickspit on its knees,
Ready to do his shadow reverence, but
A rancor curdles in its blood against
The army, which it hopes to browbeat, starve,
And cow ; yea, through the king, disband, that he
May be the pivot-point of power.   This is
The cipher of its deeds in honest speech.

They would illude us with this treaty talk.
The treaty is but verbal gossamer.
It is not meant to bind the king to aught,
But to cocoon him with a grave pretense.
Think not suspicion puts black fingers on
My eyes, blinding me to the facts ; for what
They do is too transparent to conceal
Their animus, their crystallized intent.
Now ask yourselves your duties to the realm.
As guardian of its interests, we have met
And overcome its foes ; the king himself
Its direst, deadliest foe. This closes not
Our term of office, while the danger still
Is raging as the maddened thunder roars
Among the ragged cliffs of Derbyshire,
But leaves us guardian still. As first we were
Impelled to this, in duty to the realm,
So now the tempest-beaten crest of these
Events is bearing us beyond our will ;
As though Omnipotence impels us still
To keep the course towards which we turned our prow.
Since parliament exists through us, we are
Superior to the parliament ; and right
We have to guide its hand, when laid on what
We guard. Moreover, it is instinct—ay,
Our bounden duty—to defend ourselves
Against the menace of its insolence.
We have not done offense against the realm,
Except in taking arms against the king ;
Which if the parliament shall call offense,
It stands arrayed with him, and gives the gage
To treat the two as one. Our guilt affirmed,
Let prowess gag the lie. Our innocence
Allowed, then parliament is wronging us.
In either case, we have a wrong to right.
But ask we, why it wreaks its wrath on us ?

We have not questioned its authority,
Or laid so much as one obstructive pea
Upon its path. Nay, we have been its own
Right hand in executing its behests.
Why is it spuming, then, with jealous rage?
We mean to finish what we have begun.
As God is God, you have its guidon there !
Its head has found the lap of Delilah,
And she awaits the wily Philistine.
Ay, ready is it to relinquish all
And let our sacrifices go for nought.
Say ye, with English blood a-tingling in
Your veins; say ye, as soldiers who have risked
Your all to reach a goal; say ye, as saints
Who have a covenant with God—shall this
Their insolence to us, their treason to
The realm, their daring in the face of Heaven,
Go unrebuked? For one, let Ludlow be
The servant of a dog ere that.   [*Still standing.*

   Fairfax [*Seated*].   I see
The ill but fear the remedy. A new
Confusion would not cure the old, but were
Another step towards anarchy.

    L.   Say not
A new confusion, but the old, new-fledged;
Or say, a dragon that had shed his teeth
Has got another set, with firmer fangs;
For such it is. The parliament has naught
At heart for which we fought. Naught have we gained
But what it.rates as naught. Naught do we hope
But what it dreads to see. In short, it is
The shadow of the king; and he not far
Behind.

   Ireton. Doubtless, the parliament is but
A simulated Esau, on whose hand
The kid-skin cheats the blind; while yet the voice

Is Jacob's voice. Yet fact it is, that men
Are blind ; which fact bids wariness hold check
Upon our zeal, and wait as footman at
The heels of Time.

 L.   Wait we the whims of time,
When Time waits ours. Wait, when the Devil waits.
But wait not for the people to be schooled,
When all the realm is as a smithy, where
The sputtering links, uncountable, but wait
The welding to enchain us all ; while there,
At Westminster, the witches work their spells.
The people *are* at school, and Treason holds
The rod ; at school—and learning how to spell
Out Charles ; at school—we waiting for the term
To close, when we shall be undone. Sure as
The sky is blue, a score of Colchesters,
With all the Scots to boot, are less to fear
Than this malignant parliament, which will
Not wait. Slight we our chance, 'twill turn its heel
On us.

    Enter Colonel HAMMOND.

 F. Timely as rations, colonel, to
A hungry troop.

 Hammond. A welcome thing to have
This welcome word from one whose word is more
Than welcome now.

 F.   We have relieved you of
Your onerous trust, in which your faithfulness
Has earned you this repose. You have been near
Enough the king to feel the beating of
His heart. What think you of his honesty ?

 H. Naught ; since he has no honesty to think of.

 F. What learned you of his feelings, hopes and
  plans ?

 H. In feeling, he is Charles, who, like old cheese,
Is maggoty with age. His hopes, I ween

They have the Evil One's amen.   His plans—
Nay, ask the Evil One himself.   I found
Him crammed with craft as 'twere a glutton's meal.

    F. What think you of his trial as the head
Offender of the realm.

    H.   To prove him such,
One word were so much waste.   Shall he be tried?
That question is as big as England's brain.
No wonder then it baffles mine to say.
A kindred question stands with open mouth:
Where is authority to head the head?
I see not where, unless it be the realm,
By whom, and for whom, kings exist.

    F.   You close
The question's mouth.   The realm is head ; its brain,
The Parliament ; in touching which we siege
The very capital of life : to do
Which were a venturesome temerity.

    Pride. There are emergencies that snap red-tape
As rotten tow, then take us by the throat :
And now we feel the iron gripe of such.
Who groans with toothache queries not of his
Diploma who prescribes a remedy ;
Nor yet his name who made the forceps that
Shall pull the tooth.   A cure or—farewell tooth !
Have we less wit when kingdoms are at stake ?
Shall we be casuists on the brink of doom ?
What ! haggle with our scruples as to means
Of thwarting this conspiracy, because
It wears the toggery of a parliament ?
No, not our cowardice can be a cure
For theirs who fear their duty ; neither can
It scarecrow treason.   Heroism, armed
From top to toe, is what the hour demands.

    L. The bone and marrow of the case are there.
We have the relics of a parliament,

With divers odds-and-ends picked up beside
The highway of the years, whose tenure is
Prolonged until they only represent
Themselves—a huge collective Ego, which ·
Usurps the place of power, and rules, not serves,
The realm. Now, shall we wear the shackles of
This oligarchal tyranny, which rules
Because we give it power to rule ? you have
My no, and in my heart the emphasis
Of fifty noes. I cannot brook that we,
The lawful heirs, should knee it at the feet
Of bastardy, and have it strangle us
To boot, with rope our hands have made.

II. Your action on the person of the king,
Leaves little for debate. In that, you leapt
The precipice of policy, beyond
The reach of an alternative. Seizing
The lion by the beard, you have to meet
His claws.

L.   The parliament is king's-claws to
Us ; and it threatens disembowelment.

F. One sees more ills than fifty can avert.

L. One can avert what fifty dare not face,
By waiting not to meet them face to face.
The spur of Time is in our ribs, and we
Must leap the ditch or tumble into it.
Delay we now, we cut the hamstrings of
Our opportunity. Delay we, then
I see the king restored, imperious as
A mimic Jupiter, with wrath ablaze,
And armed with bolts of terrible revenge.
I see the parliament upon its knees,
Bathing the royal feet with craven tears,
And soothing him with unctuous flatteries.
I see a gallows looming through the mist,
With baskets ready to receive our heads.

I see this army scattered like the dust,
Malignants trampling on it in contempt.
I see the realm enslaved as ne'er before.
I see all this with help now arm's length off.
These ranting rogues, these Judases, who reck
Not save to serve themselves ; who, in their craft,
Kiss with the lip while in the hand they hold
The price of liberty, must yield to those
Who serve the realm and represent its will ;
For on the open page of Providence
I see it written in large capitals.   [*Exeunt.*

SCENE II. *Army headquarters, St. Albans. Five ad-
    jutants enter carrying a petition. One reads.*

Adjutant. Respected generals! We, who represent
The army, come to lay the burden of
Its heart before your feet, full sure that, in
The fear of God, you both will hear and heed
Its earnest prayer. Serving this realm, we laid
Our lives as money in its hand, with which
To buy exemption from the tyranny
Of an ungodly king, who, not content
To king it o'er the body as no king
Before had done, would set a judgment seat
Above our souls, above our God, and judge
Us where alone the right is His. This price
We paid for liberty, as men, as saints.
In its expenditure we never called
For stint ; yet hoped we for the worth of what
We gave. In this we have been cheated to
Our face, as well you know, as never men
Before since time began, till common knaves
Might blush to see the deed and prank themselves
In presence of it as akin to saints.
Look at the cost, then seek ye the return.

Thousands on thousands felt the teeth of death
Rasping their bones, who dared him to his worst,
If so they might but leave old England free.
Thousands were mangled who are yet alive,
Whose blue-lipped scars are clamoring for redress.
Thousands lie buried like so many dogs,
Who hoped their death might earn the rights of men.
Thousands of homes have got an empty nook,
Where Grief sits brooding with a downcast eye.
And all of us have given the best we had,
To gain the best that God to man can give.
Now seek the guerdon given us in return.
Nay, go and seek the wind that blew last March !
Where is the king who flogged us with our woes ?
Fondled and slavered on by fawning knaves !
He still is full of quirks as hell of fiends ;
Yet like to have his liberty, to play
The devil where he played the imp. For all
The land is pock-marked o'er with plots for his
Release, while parliament is *parley, meant*
To smooth his passage back to power, so soon
As divers bargains can be made. Now what
Of us—we who have made it possible
To save the realm ? we who have been the shield
And breastplate of the parliament ? we who
Have looked to it as to our mother's breast ?
We are despised ; yea, hectored by it ; yea,
Refused its ear ; yea, treated as arch foes.
The brunt of its ingratitude might set
A statue's heart on fire, and fill its hot
Lips with anathemas. But add to this
Its fumy vomitings of insolence
And threat,—the dead might justly rise, donned in
Their dusty cerements, and administer
A foretaste of the horrors of the damned.
Yet have we borne it all. Borne it ? Ay, and

With patience never matched by man with like
Affront since time began. Patience ? Patience
Until we blush to think of it, and do
Abase ourselves before the Lord, and own
To you that we have been dull laggards in
Our zeal.   But we awake, and lay aside
The grave-clothes of remissness, to amend.
In doing this, we ask that you may weigh
Our just complaint, and see that parliament
Shall lay its hands upon the king, to mete
Him out the merit of his deeds, that so
The realm be unbewitched of these its woes.
To this we urge you as your souls would live.
Law for the king as for a common man.
Law for the king, to prove that law is king.
But if he breaks the law, and they connive,
Then blame us not if we be like our king.

 Fairfax. Sure godlier men and braver never faced
The crash of battle's front.   Believe me, when
I think of them it is with godly pride.
Amid the stress of strife I feel in them
The beat of victory's heart.   Such honor caps
Their bravery as is seldom won by man.
Now comes a war of self with self ; in which
I trust the victory will be theirs ; for such
A victory will encrown the rest.   Forget
Not, that we owe the parliament and realm
A loyal heart and duties manifold ;
For this, as Englishmen, ye never will
Deny.   Remember, could we stand where stands
The parliament, we might have other eyes.
Then let us do our duties as brave men,
Assured the outcome will be of the Lord.

 Ad. Two facts are blazing on our memory's walls,
As written by the hand of God.   The first :
We are the realm's backbone.   The next : *Duties*

Are written both sides of the leaf. Here, then,
The parliament has duties jointly with
The army, which, as you attest, consists
Of godly men and brave, who thus far are
The salt that saves the realm. We have not spent
These brawling years of toil, and want, and wounds,
As penny-pickers, idling to and fro ;
But, with the realm in large-hand writ upon
Our hearts, and God and Zion ever in
Our eye, we have endured what gentlemen
In parliament would suffer not to hap
Their hounds. And are we less than hounds? We
    have,
As members of the realm, whose toils and blood
Have saved it, rights which parliament may not
Despise. We have the right to ask, that they
Who never with their little finger touched
What we have borne, shall not be prodigal
Of what we purchased at so dear a rate.
We have the right to lay our burdens off,
By ridding us of that which binds them on,
And so that, once laid down, we shall not need
To take them up again. And we declare,
That as the God we serve shall stand by us,
We will. They shall not throw away the loaf
That we have made to feed this king-starved realm ;
But we will leave it to our children, and
To theirs. So say we all. [*Turning towards the others.*
  The other Ads.   We do !
  Ad.   You ask
Our bravely waiting for an *outcome* from
The Lord. The time for *in-go* has arrived :
And breaches are not lolling-places for
The brave. We cannot wait to see the done
Undone. Were Justice here in flesh and blood,
Our story poured into his ear would start

The lightning to his eye, and make him grasp
His sword ; while even Mercy, by his side,
Would read his heart and say : So mote it be.
    F. Go ye your ways. We will consider what
You say. Meanwhile, give heed that Satan tempt
You not. [*Exeunt.*] 'Tis clear the reservoir is full,
And we must find an outlet ere it leaks
And overwhelms us all. But what, advise
Ye ; and arouse your wits to meet the hour.
    Ireton. We need no abacus to reckon up
Our duty. Parliament forgets alike
Its mission and its dignity, and in
Ungodly strife seeks most ungodly ends.
Some knees are bending to propitiate
The king, whose favor their prophetic fears
Are sniveling for. Others attain not to
The level of our exigency, but
In dawdling let the time for action slip.
Still others make the parliament a rack,
On which to force the realm to sundry vain
And hybrid prelatries, who find in us
Their only obstacle ; on whom they fain
Would fix the thumbkins of the covenant,
And have us, in their livery, serve the king.
Now comes Decision's clinch, which must decide
For life or death, for us or them. I say,
We must decide, and now, or find ourselves
Betrayed by bat-blind bigots, poltroons, knaves ;
Which were stark suicide ; rank treason to
The realm ; backsliding from the Lord, whose hand
Has led us hitherto : to which, I know,
Our hearts will not consent.
    Adj-Gen. Allen.   I hear
The army as the voice of Providence, which chides
Our tardiness. For what it asks is but
The will of God ; even the saving of

This goodly realm, whose life is in our hands.
Think ye that in the reckoning day we shall
Be quit of guilt, if we despise so great
Responsibility, the like of which
Men never had since ocean licked our shores !
The very power of God is urging us ;
And as the crank of destiny is in
Our hands, so would He have us turn the winch,
To raise the realm from her besotted state.
'Twere well to help the parliament to see
Its duty, or to yield to those who do.
 Pride. I am not skilled in subtleties ; nor need
I be when Duty stands so squarely in
My path that I must rub his mantle would
I pass. We have no choice. Necessity
Has set his iron teeth and raised his whip
Behind our backs, compelling us to move.
We must not heed the syren, Policy ;
Nor ask Timidity what others think ;
Nor empty rag-shops for a precedent ;
Nor let the darkness fill our front with ghosts.
Necessity looks but one way—right on.
Resist him, he will smite us in the face.
His law is as the anchor of the hills.
Know what is necessary—that is right.
Then let our foot be as the foot of Time—
Forwards, and ever on the move, In this,
Then, is my answer : What must be, to save
The realm, must be by means that best
Will gain the end.
    Enter Members of Parliament.
 Groby.   Well met in council, since
Our ills are clamoring for a remedy.
The Presbyterians in the house are stiff
As buckram, save when thinking of the king,
When they become as pliant as one's thumb.

Their only haggle is, to squeeze him till
His conscience pukes a little prelatry
And gulps the covenant. Then would they trust
The self-same conscience, patched and pied with his
Hypocrisies, both with their heads, estates,
Souls, everything. So England has to wait
Until his conscience heaves ! The way they prate
Might give a god the colic ! Pardon the
Expression. But their doings are enough
To make an angel half forget himself.
Rivers of talk in tides that never ebb ;
As though they thought the earth might rust upon
Its axis, waiting on their whirligig
Of whims ; while traitors hatch like maggots in
July, and the great crisis hastens on
Apace.   The realm's affairs are hanging as
Upon an icicle, ready to slip
And lose us everything.
    Moore.   That, generals, is
The naked Truth.
    I.   Then Truth has need to wash
Herself.
    M.   'Twould take a sea to wash her clean.
    F. Suppose we undertake the task ?
    G.   God speed
Your loyalty ! The utmost of the law
Were mercy to the realm and worthy you.
    I. The highest law is the interpreter
Of laws. It has a constitution in
Our intuitions and necessities.
It is granitic in its quality ;
Yet may we hew it to the purpose of
The hour. To this our circumstances urge.
They who conspire against the rightful power
Are traitors, whom 'tis right to place beneath
The country's feet : a principle confessed

By parliament in taking arms against
The king. Then measure parliament by its
Own tape line, and this principle will fit
Its back. Since divers of its members have
Conspired against the realm, to serve the king,
They take the hue and character of his
Offense, and cease to be the lawful power.
Who then shall call these traitors to account ?
The powers that be, through whom they hold their
    power :
And that we are, who made them what they are.
We then must call them to condign account,
As best befits the hour's emergency.
On this the army is unanimous ;
And what it says we cannot well gainsay.

   F. We have no serrate grudges, with whose teeth
We wish to saw the parliament ; nor do
We aim to be supplanters, but to thwart
Their schemes who feel superior to the realm,
And use it as a bribe to serve their ends ;
And this as God permits, we mean to do :
For as the voice of Duty bade us pluck
The realm from ruin now it bids us keep.

   Walton. Will Cromwell stomach this ?

   F.   His stomach found
A vomit in the king, and will no more
Of him. The jaded nag prefers the short
Cut home ; and he, with us, is weary of
Delay that only gives the traitors heart.
Breathless events are stepping on our heels,
Bidding us haste. Let us retire then—three
Of you and three of us—to mold our plans,
And keep one step beyond the traitors' toes.   *[Exeunt.*

SCENE III. *A barber shop in London. Two men seated
on a bench.*

First Citizen. Heaven save us! for since England
 perched upon
The sea the like was not that army kinged
It o'er a parliament in knock-down style.
 Second Cit. Heaven needs to save from such a parlia-
 ment,
Which earns a knock-down as no parliament
Before. But heaven will save through anything
Or nothing, while it asks no odds of thee
Or me. Hence is our fuss all fudge. When foes
Are grinning in old England's face, the one
That knocks them down is Heaven's own righteous fist.
And greater foe had England never than
The king, whose craft plays devil everywhere
At once, and finds its imps in parliament.
 First Cit. Ay, curs can bark outside the lion's cage,
And be no more than curs. But let them keep
Outside, or woe betide! Armies for wars,
And kings and parliaments for laws. But Hodge
Here makes a hodge-podge of the low-bred of
The land who, perked in soldier's gear, have pranked
Themselves on wit to pick out who shall sit,
And what be done, when men of quality
Are half adaze to know.
 Second Cit.   Belike, Hodge knows
The way to pick them out. The Devil knows
Who picked them in ; but fifty might undo
Their wits to tell what good they are. Their fault
Is too much sitting when they ought to stand
And shew their backbone as the army has.
With England struggling in the whelming waves,
What want we with a lot of tongues, whose length
Would measure all the coast, with wind enough

To plague the sea? 'Tis time that some one's fist
Should fill their mouth.
  Third Cit. [Entering]. Fist—mouth. Whose fist
   and mouth?
I'll find the fist if thou the mouth, and try
The fit.
  Second Cit. Thou hast enough of mouth thyself
               [*Rising.*
For fist to fit; and here is one would like
To try thy teeth; so set thyself in trim.
  Third Cit. Nay, deck not nonsense in a parson's gown.
Thy fist would wed my mouth; but I forbid
The banns. The two are not agreed; so let
Them now, henceforth, and ever, be apart.
  Second Cit. To save thy nose let nonsense keep his
   place.   [*Sitting down.*
Beshrew me! but we pantomime the king
And parliament, craft conquering power.
  First Cit.   What, should
I play the army, gag the parliament,
And seize the king?
  Second Cit.   Proceed if thou hast right,
And thew to back it; both of which, as I
Have wit, the army has.
  First Cit.   Nay, bar its right
In face of ancient English law, to which
We must defer as to the will of God.
  Second Cit. What! must we seek the midnight and
   the tombs;
Invite the ghosts to leave their ancient graves,
And have them king us now, with iron rule?
What vested rights has such like shadowy stuff
In our material things? Who makes us liege
To brains long turned to dust? What power is in
The memory of their deeds to force our deeds?
Nay, let the Past present its capias first,

And drag us to its bar to answer there.
Till then we may defy the dust of all
The kings—their ghosts to boot—and brush away
The must and mildew of the years. The quick
To serve the quick, the dead the dead.

  First Cit.   There must
Be something solid and immovable,
On which to rest our liberties ; and on
That rock the king or parliament must build.
The king forbidden, parliament remains.
But here the army meddles, void of right.

  Third Cit. Suppose thou box the army's ears and set
It on a stool, to meditate and suck
Its thumb.

  Second Cit. From whence has parliament its power ?
Itself ? Then let it save itself. The realm ?
Then let it serve the realm. Prythee, dissect
The realm and tell its bones, and may be thou
Wilt find the army is its backbone, whose
Support is needful, that the head may keep
Its poise. Ask, Whence the army ? From the realm.
For what ? To save us from a king who deemed
Us slaves. But here thou sticklest at the means
That reach no end save what the realm designed,
And in no way save what necessity
With fescue pointed out : for thou would'st save
Our liberties. Our liberties ! And here
These tinkers, in their law-shop, blow the fire
Of treason, with their solder near, to patch
Up matters with the king, undoing so
What took the realm and army years to do.
No, these are not the tricks of liberty.

  Third Cit. Yea, Liberty a-standing on her head—
A mountebank upon a shaky stage,
Which any day may fall and let her down.
But whether now on head or feet she be,

Old Nick may guess.

Second Cit. This realm is owned by king
Nor parliament.

First Cit. Nor army.   .

Second Cit. Even so ;
But mistress, who no master owns but God,
Her rights are as the texture of her soul,
Inwoven in her being by His hand.

Fourth Cit. [*Entering*]. A parson here. Amen !
The text—chapter
And verse.

Third Cit. The chapter is, the chap who lost
A crown ; the verse, what tells how divers fools
Went down to Jericho ; the subject, Pride,
Which goes before a fall.

Fourth Cit. Good soul ! thou hast
Not slept in sermon time, as children do.
But is the fifty-ninth and lastly gone,
And the *improvement* thinned off to a close ?

First Cit. Thou art a dull-wit or a care-for-naught,
To sit astride destruction with a grin.

Fourth Cit. A grin or groan, the jade will keep her
jog ;
And so I grin and save a doctor's bill.

Second Cit. Fool or philosopher, thy speech would fit
The mouth.

Fourth Cit. Which proves it is a fitting speech.

Second Cit. It were not fit that all should have thy
speech.

Fourth Cit. Lest they become philosophers—goose-
necked,
With nose that seeks the ground ?

First Cit. Thy magpie wit
Has got a slit-tongue readiness.

Third Cit. [*A man rushing in*]. Odds zounds !
A whirlwind on two legs, a goblin in

The rear.

    Fifth Cit. Cromwell is here.

    Third Cit.   I see him not.

    Fifth Cit. At Westminster ; and pats the army on
The back for having ousted parliament.

    First Cit. And would had Pride cut all our throats.

    Fourth Cit.   Why not ?
For then were fewer throats to gulp the king.

    Fifth Cit. Cromwell is right since right the army did.
Think of it, snubbed, robbed, starved, challenged to
Its face, by gouty gentlemen who thought
They carried England in their fob, and but
Consulted her to know their dinner time.
For once their mightinesses overreached
Their wits ; as now they find.

    Fourth Cit.   And, ten to one,
They had not much to overreach. And now,
I ween, they stand upon their dignity
As pegtops on their point.

    Second Cit.   Cromwell approves
The course pursued ?

    Fifth Cit.   Yes, on the word
Of one who overheard a member say.

    Second Cit. Great men can enter the arcana of
Events and see the soul of things, while most
But grope and guess around the bodied form.
Hence those have an impulsion towards a goal
Where others think chimeras lure astray.
'Tis this divinest instinct of the man
That shews us whitherward the destinies
Are drifting us—ay, shapes the destinies.
Here Cromwell is a king ; while he once king
Has proved himself a lout. One looks Time in
The eye and reads his heart. The other fails
To understand his plainest speech. Hence one
Is master of events ; the other, slave.

Fifth Cit. The king is Scot in blood, an Irishman
In heart, a papist through and through, and fool
From toe-nail to the end of every hair.

 First Cit. Ten years ago that speech had cost thee
  dear.

 Third Cit. I see not why when heads were cheap as
  dirt.

 Fifth Cit. In sooth, the market had a good supply
Of better heads than ours. Now we shall be
Content to get a king's.

 First Cit.   Hush thou !   Behead
A king ? Make England's coffin if it comes
To that. Methinks the very axe would shrink
And chide the lifted hand ; yea, and the block
Be seized with horror and refuse his neck.

 Fourth Cit. An arrow did not shun good Harold's eye,
A king whose toe were worth the head of Charles ;
Nor block refuse the necks of Harry's queens,
Whose virtues are not in this mongrel's blood.

 First Cit. To kill a king would be the king of crimes.
It comes near grazing very Deity.
Confess infirmity that makes him man.
There is divinity that makes him king.
Strike we the man, we strike infirmity ;
But strike the king, we strike divinity.

 Fifth Cit. Jack Ketch would take no more, I ween,
  than just
His head who fathers the infirmity,
Leaving divinity to help itself.

 Second Cit. Divinely blind, and now divinely weak ;
What pity but he were content to be
A man. The bladder is too small to hold
The wind of his divinity.

 Fifth Cit.   Hark ye !
The tramp of soldiers in the street. Away ! [*Exeunt.*

SCENE IV. *The House of Commons.*

Pride. I have been asked, within a day, the source
Of my authority for what is done.
See these,—[*Circling his hands towards the generals and
     others*],—in whom is more of wit to rule
Than fifty bastard parliaments—and there
You see the *brain* of my authority.
Look at the army—which has loyalty
Enough to guarantee the safety of
The realm—and there you find the *backbone* of
The same authority.   Or ask you more ?
Behold the wounds of this distracted land—
The wounds whose festering might evoke a groan
From every stone upon her streets.   In them
Resides the *soul* of my authority.
Turn to Humanity and read the laws
Inscribed upon her heart, by fingers of
Infinity, and know : Eternity
Gives *common law* for my authority.
If others can outweigh it, let us hear.
     Ireton. Authority !   England and England's God
Are our authority.   And as they rule,
So we shall wield it as they will.   And let
A dog bark at Omnipotence rather
Than Treason wag his tongue.   Authority !
Who gave this parliament authority ?
Not Charles—though none more readily than they
Would lick his hand—for he was in duress
When half assumed their seats.   Not England—though
They took her name in vain, to gloze their deeds—
For not enough to form a regiment
Could tell their whence or how.   And not the Lord—
Whose name to know, belike, they had to mouth
An oath—for every step of theirs has been
With cloven foot.   Then let not them demand

Authority. We represent the realm—
Some in, all out of, parliament. To us
It gave a unique work, in doing which
We found these renegades across our path-;
Whom, from necessity, we clear away.
Now lies before us what the realm requires—
The final stroke that shall insure her peace;
A stroke I need not name: for, as you know,
To what we put our hand, you know to what
We owe the final touch. The king is first
And last, body and soul, of all the ills
Whose pestilential power has smitten us;
Which ills will last until he breathes his last.
To duty, then, as we regard the realm,
And would approve our conscience, and endure
His gaze who flinches not when justice bids.
   Cromwell. I ask not of authority. Who has
A better let him give us better deeds.
I speak of principles, whose roots are in
The law that is the subsoil of all laws
Whose fruits are righteousness. Then note ye **this**:
Law heads the king or he the law. But law
Has made him king. Then law is head, and he
Is liege. Hence kings, in *Magna Charta* and
The Bill of Rights, have kneed it to the law.
But now a Stuart breaks, contemns, defies
The law, and so rebels against the head;
Which treason, in the highest subject of
The law, is highest treason known to law—
The treason of a ruler to his trust;
A recreance to the body of the head:
Which threatens all on which our weal depends.
For, if so arch a traitor miss his dues,
All villainies will prank themselves and feel
Secure. No, law should be maintained; **and they**
Maintain who gave it parentage, whose will

Is as the Providence of kings. 'Tis here
The timid cast the lead-and-line, to find
An anchorage in precedents, but find,
Instead, an ocean bottomless ; because
No precedential exigence has left
A chart for needy mariners. We have
An interregnum with a king ; a king
Who has become the phantom of himself ;
A no-king, who excludes a regency.
Then what is treason, who are traitors now ?
What threats, and they who threat, the interests of
The realm to serve their individual ends ;
As did malignants here in parliament,
Who were compounding with the common foe.
What now is law, and who shall execute ?
The general will, and those who represent
That will to serve its weal ; which will resolved
Itself into organic force : which force
We are. Here then are our credentials for
Our deeds. And now, as God hath borne us in
The chariot of His power, from strength to strength,
To work His will, so we proceed to do.
Hence we demand, that he who broke shall face
The law and feel its penalty. And it
Behooves to oil the wheels of time with our
Alacrity. Delay abets his hopes ;
And while we slumber treason plays the thief.
This business done a year ago had saved
A lake of blood ; deferred, 'twill cost a sea.
There is no reason why we should defer,
While all the nerves of Patience are unstrung ;
But every reason clamors, Expedite
And help to blot the shame of past delay.
Alas ! that shame is ineffaceable ;
Since written in the choicest English blood.
Still, let us—since fate's ratchet on the wheels

Of time keeps back the past—bid sloth begone,
And weak timidity ; confess our fault,
And by our promptitude atone, if such
Can be, grasping the axe as we have grasped
The sword.

   Fairfax. What we have done is rightly done ;
Nor, could we, would we that it were undone ;
For, rightly done, it has the seal of Heaven :
A seal that it were sacrilege to break.
We took the gage in championing the law.
We measured lances, and the foe is thrown.
Now we would not be stricken in the back.
Blame us in this the *last*—ye blame yourselves,
Who bade us give the *first* cut at the band
That bound the king and parliament ; ye blame
Us that the stroke ye ordered found the hilt.
But no ; I ween you will not blame us now
Because our loyalty has kept its edge,
To cut as keenly as in earlier strokes.
Treason alone will blame ; and that we beard ;
Nor will we give it quarter, as we live.

   Bradshaw. Law's primal principles are precedent
Enough for what is done. We need not seek
The footprints of our sires before we step.
The path of progress is not in our rear.
They trod the way of liberty ; and we
Continue whence they parted hands. The law
Of progress is at once our precedent,
Behoof, necessity, and right. Treason
May hold his ear against the keyhole of
The past, and hear the mumblings of its ghosts,
And spells of witches, jingling manacles,
And clanking chains. But we need neither halt
Nor be bewitched ; neither accept the one
Nor wear the other. Why debate ? We have—
In making war—assumed, yea, set ourselves,

A precedent; for by the sword we called
The king to an account before the law;
And by his treating with us he has owned
Our right to offer terms: in doing which,
We claimed the right to start, and he has owned
The competence of law to close the strife.
Thus both acknowledge law as arbiter.
Since we prefer the charge, 'tis ours to state
Its nature and extent, and his to meet
It as he may; which right we exercised
In formulating erst the charge, serving
In War's most sanguinary mode; while now,
As sheriff of the realm, the army holds
The prisoner in duress. This then remains
Our sole alternative—to prosecute,
Or give account for that already done.
For either he is traitor to the realm,
Or we are traitors to the king. Now, not
To prosecute would be to own our guilt,
And so to make ourselves amenable:
A thing that none of us is anxious for.

 C. Action stands breathless at the open door
Of opportunity, waiting our word.
Speak one and all; and let our heart be in
The word, an undertone of honesty.
Yea, speak, and let insulted Patience dry
Her tears, as Action leaps the threshold here
To-day. Do we our duty, counting not
The cost, assured the Lord will pay the bill:
For as He has approved our course, He will.
Appoint a court, then, that shall try the king—
A special court to meet a special need—
And deal him as his deeds have duly earned.

 B. The realm is Heaven's vicegerent in the case.
Behind whose will no earthly power may stand.
Hence has she sole adjudicatory right,

Which none may dictate how to exercise.
Courts are of her, and for her, as she wills.
A special need demands a special court,
Which here she may ordain and constitute.
Then I approve a court to try the king.
Do what we do apertly, in her name ;
And let his innocence give answer, if
It can, or let his guilt receive its dues.
The wronged has right to vindicate her rights. [*Exeunt.*

SCENE V. *Farnham Castle.* CHARLES *and* WARWICK
alone.

Charles. Deciduous fortune sheds its leaves, and I
Am shelterless in this the winter of
My woe. What men have dwelt within these walls,
Whose varied fortune symbolizes mine !
This pile, with eyes and heart, might groan to see
Its master's plight. Would he had none for what
He sees and feels ! Draw nearer, Warwick. Thou,
To-night, art all the world to me ; since all
Besides is utter vacancy, devoid
Of interest as the ashes of one's hopes.
I feel a strange foreboding of my fate—
The essence of a melancholy that
Is poison to the soul.
    Warwick [*Caressing the king's hand*]. Your Majesty
Is weary from the drive on rack-joint roads ;
And in the stress of flesh the spirit flags.
The dew of sleep distilled upon your nerves
Will make the morning fresh with opening flowers.
    C. 'Tis more than weariness, and deeper than
The joints. It is an inkling to the soul,
That Mephistopheles has waved his wand
Across their hearts whose red hands rule the hour.

W. Were foul diabolism hot within
There would be fumes of brimstone in the speech.

        Enter Major HARRISON.

    C. There have been smothered whispers in my ear
Of an intent that dares not hear itself
Speak out.

    Harrison. What meaning couches there ?

    C.   There has
Been profanation of my person with
Impunity, begetting madness that
Would sate itself with royal blood.

    H.   There is
A reverence for the laws which means to let
You meet them face to face.

    C.   They dare not that.
Mark me. I say, They dare not that. There is
A daring that has Desperation for
Its father, and for mother, Recklessness.
It is begotten, born, matured, and has
A gleaming dagger in its hand, to do
In darkness what it dares not in the light.
It loves the blood of innocence ; hence has
It thirst for mine.

    H.   Think not the parliament
Will skulk behind a hedge to do what it
Has warrant for in law. So just its cause,
It wants that justness written legibly
Upon the page that generations con.

    C. A morning rainbow spans its troubled heart,
Reflected on the background of its fears,
And gives its face a smirk of confidence.
But in that background lurks a storm ; for such
Is nature, that its deepest feelings will
Direct its deeds.

    H.   I hope you measure not
Your coat to know the size of parliament.

But, be assured, it would rejoice to have
The world's eye, as the noonday sun, look down
On what it does. For my part, what I do
Shall have no squint in line with lydford law.
With this, good night.   ·   [*Exit.*

    C.   How big, to prattle to
A king and play the malapert ! And what
A chance a rushlight of authority
Affords to shew his peacock plumes !—Law—law !
A jackdaw croaking in his master's ears
Of law. And they will condescend to give
A king fair play ! A midge will deign to speak
To Jupiter ! My hopes may pillow on
A traitor's word ! No. Nothing in his deeds
Or theirs would make me trust the word.
For evil lurks, as ghosts in darkness, in
An evil heart, fearing the light. What boots
The bending of the knee in mockery ?
The decking with a dirty purple robe ?
The plaiting of a crown of thorns, which is
But meant to pierce me to the quick ?—And yet,
Who knows but it betrays their fears ? The brute
Has but brute motives at the best.

    W.   In sooth,
Your Majesty, they are a brutish herd.
And yet, methinks, their merest instinct would
Suggest, that foul means for your taking off
Would shake in shudders through old England's blood,
Making her heart like Afric's stormy cape—
Where halcyon never spreads her sky-tint wing—
And whelm them in the billows of revenge.

    C. Ah, Warwick ! thou dost credit them with sight
And attributes of men ; whereas they are
Bat-blind—so blind that Reason cannot give
Them sight ; and, destitute of reverence, they
Are lacking its component parts ; in which

They lack the sense of honor, truth, and the
Etceteras of the gentleman.   Perchance,
The Great Supreme has let their passions loose,
To leave a warning on the shores of time,
Like headland beacons on a treacherous coast,
For upstarts who would be piratic kings.

    W. There is an instinct in the brute to cling
To life ; and this they have in common with
The brute, in such degree as proves their more
Than brutishness.   Whence I infer, that they
Will have the semblance of a court, to save
Themselves the odium of their deeds, and give
The public wrath extinguishment.

      C.   A court !
A king arraigned before his subjects !   Me,
Whom they have hid these years lest men should see
Their king and prove their loyalty !   Let them
Attempt it and the very world would rise.
It were to set the subject o'er the king ;
To stand a pyramid upon its apex ;
To have a shears-and-lapstone government :
A plague that might inoculate the world.
Hence is it that my case would be the world's.
But they can scent a danger nearer home.
Full well they know, that did the people see
Their king, the heart of England would be wild
A-leap.   Hence, like a smuggled prize, they keep
Me well concealed.   Their quandary is as when
The baited bull, to guard both ends at once,
Lunges in desperation at the dogs.
It is the lunging policy I dread.
Be that escaped, I still have three cards left,
The worst of which will give back everything.

    W. A threefold happy fact, if fact it be.

    C. Your if is needless as a second nose.
The hopes of Ireland hang upon my skirts ;

And she could turn the balance trembling here.
Denmark is not forgetful of the past ;
Nor France unfearful of a precedent.
Indeed, the world is waking to perceive
A solidarity of interest ; that
The thrones are all a fascine : take out one
We loosen all. If only we could steal
A slice of time !

    W.   'Twere both a timely and
An honest theft.

    C.   Time is our all, our life ;
And now the guaranty of life ; for in
Its web are all the threads of destiny.

        Enter Bishop of London.

Bishop. May God be gracious to your Majesty !
Newburgh, of Bagshot, has a heart to serve ;
And, can you visit him, will prove the same.

    C. You bring a primrose from the winter's breast.
England is all blue sky ; and loyal hearts
Are stars, besprinkled everywhere. But clouds
Exclude the splendor of their sheen. Thank him,
Most reverend lord, and tell him I would fain
Accept his service could he serve me—me
Whose movements are no more my own.

    B. [*Handing a letter to Charles*]. He can.
Therein, I ween, is ample evidence.

    C. [*Reading*]. Bagshot ! The key of liberty, of hope,
Of everything. [*Rising and pacing the floor.*] We must
        to Bagshot, if
The purpose of the escort can be swerved.

    W. Moonlike, my heart receives the rapture of
Your Majesty's, reflecting back your joy.
What tidings thrill you so ?

    C.   A prospect of
Escape. How that would take their impudence
Aback !

W.   Heaven grant it may be feasible !

B. This may be Heaven's appointment to rebuke
Their rank impiety, and shew the world
That royalty can leave the furnace, though
'Tis seven times hotter than its wont, without
The smell of fire.   Heaven's own anointed has
Heaven's guardian arm about his path.

   C. [*Sitting down*].   More true
Has never passed your lordship's lips.   The crown
Despised ; my subjects up in arms ; myself
The prey of rogues ; domestic ties disrupt ;
To-day all dark ; to-morrow deep in fog ;
Looking into the very throat of death,—
This sevenfold heat was ne'er before so hot.
But there is One—my conscience—like the Son
Of man, who walks with me amid the flames,
And gives their tips a beatific touch.

   B. Your holy innocence inspires your tongue
With heavenly seasoned eloquence.   Heaven must
Be near a soul so like to heaven ; and, doubtless, it
Has heavenly boon in store.

   C.   I must
Communicate with Harrison to stop
At Bagshot.   Bid him—or invite him—here.   [*Exit W.*
What more contemptible than fallen kings,
Who ask the favors it is theirs to give !
No cur so small but he may have his bark.
But stars will fall, and suns will set ; those lost
Forever, these to rise again.   So may
I rise, and so shall traitors fall.

       Enter HARRISON *and* WARWICK.

   H.   What wills
Your Majesty ?

   C.   To stay at Bagshot, where
His lordship, Newburgh, will be proud to give
Accommodations worthy of a king :

A souvenir of hopeless loyalty.

H. To Bagshot? But we cannot linger there.

C. I ask no more than time for needed rest,
To taste the sweets of hospitality,
Among the leafy glories of its woods,
And warm one heart before the fire goes out.

H. With Windsor in our view it may be done.

C. I ask no more. [*Exit Harrison.*] How freely
    one can give
A gem who knows not what he gives! But what
Chagrin to learn its worth when lost! This game
Will stand their projects on their heads. There may
They stay till the projectors have no heads!

W. It does indeed afford a vista to
Your hopes, if naught shall trip the scheme.

C.   Warwick,
Thy ifs are thorns that grow with every rose.

W. All roses have their thorns; and keen are those
Whose points have pierced your Majesty.

C.   True as
The lisp of Truth in infant innocence,
Save that the primrose breaks the thorny rule.

W. The *evening* primrose means Inconstancy,
The twin of If, and thorn of thorns withal.

C. Full true, alas; for they have been the right
And left hand that have meted out my dole.

Enter a Servant. *Hands a letter to* WARWICK *at the
                  door.*

Servant. A letter by a secret messenger,
Whose haste well nigh betrayed him to the guard.

W. [*Handing it to the king.*] A letter. Happy be
    its broach!

B.   God grant
A gracious boon!

C. [*Reading*]. My worst prophetic fears
Fulfilled!

B.   Heaven save your gracious Majesty !
I hope and pray the worst is past.

C.   No doubt.
Such fangles are my heritage. Turn hopes
And prayers to gold, my wealth, ere this, had put
The Indies to the blush. It is the fate
Of hapless kings to have redundant help
From impotent officiousness.

B.   Be calm.
Your Majesty takes too, too much to heart
The passing of a cloud that blurs your sky.
Indeed you do. Look you around, above.
Or if events have wearied you, then close
Your eyes and rest. These sudden humors of
The flesh afflict the spirit with a long
Concatenation of despondencies,
Which work it ill. His lordship has a plan
For your escape which is most feasible ;
Of which you are to some extent apprized.

C. As feasible as sowing moonshine for
A crop. A lightning-footed horse, to bear
Me off, gets kicked and cannot bear himself.
What schemes that hang a kingdom on a thread !

B. Heaven's mercy ! what mishaps belong to life !
It is a bundle of uncertainties ;
And any hour may cut the cord that binds.
Is that my lord of Newburgh tells you so ?

C. About uncertainties ? He tells about
A certainty that certainly has left
Me in uncertainty.

B.   Yes, that about
The horse. Who knows the pranks of Time? He lays
A cornucopia at our feet, when lo !
Before we empty it, it vanishes.

C. The best of homilies would ill befit
This hour. But I would find myself alone. [*Exeunt.*

Here now remains whom only I may trust
                            [*Pacing the floor.*
In heart and head. Yet have I trusted heart
And head that failed me in the crucial hour.
There is my weakness ; for I own myself
Most weak in trusting most untrusty men.
No odds—the head without the heart to will
Me well, or heart without the head to work
Me well. Both are alike untrusty—twin
Abortions to necessity. I must
Re-crown, control, assert, enforce myself.
Both heart and head must do obeisance to
The king, or not demand of subjects what
The king denies himself. Charles Stuart ! mount
Thy throne of selfhood. Be a real king—
A king in kingliness of purpose, in
Inflexibility of will, in grip
To hold the opportunities, and in
Vicariate divinity, to do
Divinely where the human fails. Enough.
My deepest instincts answer with a pledge.
It shall be so. By heaven, it shall be so !—
But Nature whispers through the avenues [*Sitting down.*
Of sense, inviting sleep. Come, charmer, come.
Come—come. [*He sleeps. A pause. Warwick enters.*
   W. [*Charles awaking*]. I feared the silence boded
     hap of ill.
   C.   Whatever haps is ill. Ill is
Indigenous and, in the summer of
My wakefulness, is bannered like
The forest with its leaves, while wintry sleep
Supplies its roots with nourishment, in dreams.
   W. Let not my royal master lack in heart,
While drawing nearer to the country's heart.
   C. Ah, Warwick ! even kings are cowards when
The circumstances strike their weakest side.

But thou hast touched a chord that comforts me.
I have the country's heart ; and having that,
In London once, I shall be all myself,
And bid these kennel-littered louts exeunt.
I will compose myself and wait events.
When angels come they seek us, not we them. [*Exeunt.*

SCENE VI. *The House of Commons.*

Cromwell. The lords refuse to try the king.   Note ye
What this imports : not disagreement in
A verdict, but a verdict in advance ;
That either he is by the laws acquit,
Or is not answerable to the laws ;
By which they put themselves above the laws,
While setting us at naught. Such arrogance
We must, as men, rebuke ; as guardians of
The realm, resist, or do dishonor to
Ourselves ; to it, a treasonous wrong. Who are
These kingish mightinesses that would take
Us by the ears? Who but malignants, in
Whose every drop of blood is venom rank
Enough to kill a people's liberties ?
Who but a fledging brood, from despots who,
For centuries, picked the country's bones, when he
Of Normandy had first pecked out her eyes ?
Here, now, they claim as their prerogative—
In perpetuity and unimpaired—
The right to craunch the bones without a nay.
In sooth, their sympathies and interests, as
A class, are alien to our wishes, ways,
And weal. They are non-English at the core.
Because the breath of their abnormal life
Is breathed into their nostrils by the king,
They fawn before him and ignore the realm.
Thus would they lay Oblivion's hand upon

The years, to blot out blood and memory of
The past. Oblivion's hand ! Oblivion for
The king's malfeasances, and gibbets for
The representatives of England, of
The laws, of progress, of humanity.
But no ! These royal lickspits may not filch
From us the guerdon that it cost such blood
To gain. Lick we the dust from Charles's feet
Rather than be but carrion for his dogs.
These supernumerary somnambulists
May be informed that England, who is wide
Awake, defers not to the drowsy nod
Of their dictation, nor desires assent
To what she does. She can dispense with this
Bi-cameral device, by which these warts,
Or parasites, upon the royal skin,
Cling to the carcass that has battened them.
Who dared to call the master to account
Will not crouch craven at his minions' feet.
But, not to make my thunder of the wind,
I move that we proceed without the lords.
Ask not for precedents that tyrants forged
Amid the smoke of a vulcanic age ;
For not a wrong but it is gewgawed o'er
With them. No tenon-precedent can fit
The case ; since not a mortise-precedent
Is there to match. Since earth first whirled upon
Her axis like was never known. The king
Assumed to be as God, exempt from law.
The lords, with us, rebuked his arrogance,
Arrested him and placed him in duress.
Now they would stultify themselves and us,
Stopping their ears when he is asked to plead,
And bidding us acquit. Acquit, and say
That he is innocent ? Acquit, and brand
Ourselves as traitors all these years ? Acquit,

And relegate the realm to him who was
Its bane ?   Acquit, and justify the deeds
That made the very heart of Justice bleed?
Acquit, and gather up, and weld, and wear
Again the chains we burst and cast away ?
This they would have ; but this we will not give.
No ! never, while a drop of English blood
Is left to quicken us.   Our course was just,
And is, and so shall be maintained ; and what
Remains to do shall find its precedent
In what is done ; which had the lords' assent :
For trial is the sequence of arrest.
They helped us into this, to leave us now
To help ourselves.   And so we will, and stand
By Justice as he stands by us.
 Ludlow.   The land
Is foul with blood—blood that the king has spilt.
Then let him brave the brunt of consequence
And blot out blood with blood.   I ask no lords'
Authority for what we do.   We have
Authority from Him the Lord of lords.
To Him comes next the people, as of old,
Ere Israel lusted after heathen ways.
When these are speaking kings must bare their heads.
Tis now they speak ; then now the king must doff.
Let lords stand by and snuff, and yet beware
Lest they exceed their tether.   Law at last
Is throned.
 Bradshaw.   Preceding action of the lords
Avows the king amenable to law,
Or their resistance had been treason else.
Resisting, they condemned him of offense
Against the laws, which, by arresting, they
Apprise him to confront.   Now, they refuse
Arraignment at its bar.   What must be done?
Either the laws must be enforced or set

At naught. The latter must not be. But how
The former yet remains. The lords have gone
So far that, in retreating, they condemn
Themselves as in contempt of duty, hence,.
As cowardly : and cowardice to-day
Is treason to the realm. Thus is the realm
Betrayed ; which leaves but us between its weal
And woe. Should we be false as they, then what
Both they and we invoked the people to
Resent, and branded as high crimes, would leave
The ashes of their ignominy and
Be rampant in their utter wantonness.
One only question, then, remains : have we
The courage to arraign the prisoner for
His crimes and execute the laws, or shall
Old England's only hope prove traitor with
The rest ? Shall the uplifted dagger cleave
Her heart, or we avert the blow ? To that
This day will give its answer.

   Ireton.   Answer ! I
Can feel an answer hot in every drop
Within my veins. Ireton my name, the ire
Of righteousness is in my blood. Justice
Is what we want, and Justice we must have.
The laws are king nor must they be dethroned ;
But he, their arch transgressor, must account
To them. No time is this for shuffling off
Responsibility ; no time for quirks
To elbow duty from our path ; no time
To ease our grasp on what these years have seized ;
No time to shrink from vindicating what
Is done. But since the lords have shewn their backs,
'Tis ours to shew the bolder face. Where quail
The cowards let the brave step in. We yet
May have to try the lords. Ay, let my words
Ring out until they sting their ears. No time

Is this to use electuaries ; but
It asks a drastic remedy.   Then let
The lords be circumspect ; for Justice is
A dangerous toy to play with.
   Harrison.   I have seen
And heard the king's deceits to surfeiting.
He has a plausibility that wins
The weak, as sunshine opens flowery eyes.
Perchance, the glitter of his royalty's
Glamour dazzles as does the serpent's eye.
But those who can outstare him, see profounds
Of treachery where the venom lies ; treachery
That our surveillance has increased.   As well
Hunt shadows in a fog as honesty
In him.   Yet can his tongue be smooth—to cut
The more.   And many lords, I ween, have been
Emasculated by its lancet edge.
Beware of him.   There is a something in
His atmospheric presence that portends
A storm ; from which our covert is the laws.
A storm, I say ; of which this action of
The lords is a precursive sign.   Let us
To covert, then, and so outwile his wiles.
   C. What inkling has escaped the leash of his
Reserve ?
   H.   Less in his tongue's dubieties
Than in the nakedness of deeds.   Secrets
In soft susurrus wafted to his ear ;
Solicitude to meet with divers lords,
Whose very names caused his auroral hopes
To light his face with unctuous confidence,
Which gave his voice a fitful bravery ;
The old pretension to divinity
Re-emphasized, and the rent veil between
His sanctity and us revamped ; these and
A residue of minor indices,

Conjunctive with the action of the lords,
Betrayed collusion in a general scheme.
The rent veil, I have said. And such it was,
Until I saw the ark of royalty
Beyond ; which is a bandbox, bursting-full
Of fripperies—a sacred relic of
A heathen age—from which, no doubt, the lords
Are hoping for a periapt.
 Sidney.   To gain
Our goal we must not run with bandaged eyes.
'Tis meant to rid us of the king. What then ?
Methinks 'twould make old England's blood run cold
With ague-horror, and return to us
In fever's raging fire. A commonwealth
May be when circumstances joint the times.
But royal blood would add no strength to it.
Then spare his blood ; but paralyze his power.
Prudence has greater potency than wrath.
Expunge his title, we will cipher him ;
For Charles, as Charles, were naught.
 C.   Sir Algernon !
I am astonished—yea, surprised, amazed,
To see your prudence run amuck in this
Imprudent way. When done, no dog will bark.
Facts have solidity that even fools
Will recognize. Hence we propose to end
Uncertainty and close the argument
With fact. You think the realm would have the sword
Of justice rust. I tell you nay. 'Tis sick
At heart to see the Janus-facedness
And paltering of the king, and sick of us
For shivering on the brink of duty when
We ought to plunge.
 Groby.   We have the right ; and right
It is to do the right. The king is wrong ;
And wrong it cannot be to punish wrong.

The laws have been defied—as e'en the lords
Admit—and must assert themselves through the
Supremest legal power; which now we are.
The technical conceits that pettifog,
And carp, and stickle for the red-tape that
Would strangle Justice, must not make us swerve
Or hesitate.   Who now would spare the king
Ignores the laws, and so betrays the realm ;
And so opposes God, who made and guards
The realm ; and so is under ban, both of
His country's laws and God's almightiness.
Heaven save us from the treason of the lords !

C. Such hours as these inspire heroic souls,
And drive the craven like affrighted hares.
Let us, agreed, be heroes in our deeds,
And so escape eternal obloquy,
Which would be earned should we be falterers now.
The ages never gave a holier task,
A grander sweep of opportunities,
To mortal man than here is offered us.
Let not our cowardice belittle us
And dub us pigmies of a giant age.
I move that we proceed without the lords ;
And let them shiver in their loneliness.

Walton. The Ruler of the earth has shut us up
To this procedure, that Timidity
May have a stouter heart and force the realm
Into the forefront as the plaintiff, that
The king may see what back received his blows.
It is The People—*versus*—Charles.   Then let
Him face a bleeding realm, and learn that no
Collusion with the lords can parry justice.
Hence I support the motion to proceed.   [*Exeunt.*

SCENE VII. *St. James's Palace. Present,* HERBERT, *the* Bishop of London, *and others.* *Enter* Duke of GLOSTER *and* ELIZABETH, *with* Attendants.

Gloster [*Kissing*]. O father! will they kill you as
    they say?

Charles. Yea, child. They always keep their word
    in what
Is ill; and this is ill enough for them
To keep it now.

    G.   I wonder why it is
That badness has no check, but good men have
To die. How *can* they kill a king, when it
Were almost killing God?

    C.   God has a bunch
Of keys called *Whys*, which hang beyond our reach.
Could we but take them down, we might unlock
A haunted room and wish ourselves away.

    G. Oh, what will mother say to this, or what
We do when left alone with wicked men?

    C. Heaven help thee! Break not now a father's
    heart.

    G. No, no! I fain would mend it so that it
Should never have a crack, but, like a top,
Jump round and round.

    C.   A filial wish, welling
From nature's fount. But wishes are no more
Than heart-hands reaching for the flowers beyond
Their grasp. My son, thou now canst give my heart
A balm to sooth its dying hour.

    G.   You need
But name it and my heart will jump to do
The deed, e'en should you ask the melting of
The marrow in my bones to make a salve.

    C. Thou mindest what I said at Hampton Court
About them kinging thee?

G.   I do ; and what
I said is deeper in my heart, till I
Could wish myself a toad, to poison who
Might touch my warty skin to make me king.

    C. That stick to thee, like grace to infant souls
When passed the font, and all the unction that
A father's memory hath will rest upon
Thy soul.

    G.   Let them with pincers pull me, tooth
By tooth and bone by bone, and chop my flesh
Like Christmas mince ; but every tooth would cry,
Slack not ; and every bone, Pull on ; while the
Last bit of flesh defied them and refused
To be a king.

    Bishop.   Thou hast the mettle of
A king.   [*Aside.*

    C.   God grant thy brother Charles as brave
A heart !

    G.   Does God give hearts ?

    C.   Good hearts are gifts
Of His.

    G.   I would he had some for the men
Who want your life.

    C.   He wills to let them have
Their way, to learn at length, perchance, how bad
They are.

    G.   They ought to see it now. Can you
                  [*To the Bishop of London.*
Not tell them, bishop, what a dreadful thing
It is to kill a king ?

    B.   Nay, if they kill
The master they will give the servant but
An adder's ear.

    G.   What kind of ear is that ?

    B. An ear that will not heed.

    G.   That kind they have,

Or they would hear the thumping of my heart
Cry out for pity.

C.   Come, my daughter ; let
Me see thy face and find thy mother's lips -
In thine. [*They embrace and kiss.*] Dear innocent !
  How pale thou art !
And what dark wrinkles where the waves of grief
Have beaten on the beaches of thine eyes !
Care has devoured the sweet and tender chit
Of thy susceptive heart. The legacy
Thy father leaves is but his blessing and
The memory of his woes. But they may be
Thy soul's best wealth. When I am gone, keep thou
The image of this heaven-dewed hour beside
Thy heart to sanctify thy loneliness.
Remember, that thou wert a lily on
The bosom of his thoughts, yielding a sweet
Perfume.

E.   The world is lonesome—lonesome as
An empty room whose echoes startle one.
How can I say good-by ? O Heaven ! that earth
Should have so little heart !

C.   This is the death
Of Death. The death that follows this will but
Be undertaker to my poor remains.

E. What will the world be worth when you are gone ?

C. O darling ! God and duty will remain
To thee. Keep thou thy heart beneath Heaven's light,
That so the petals of its purity
May open with a noontide loveliness
And shew the sunflame glowing in its life.
Seek thou thy mother. Tell her—oh, my lords !

        [*Weeping.*
The arrow sticks.   [*A pause.*

G.   Oh ! I could kill them all !

         [*Sobbing.*

C. Nay, say not so.   And yet—poor child !   Nat
Will mock our prim moralities.   Tell thou   [*T*
Thy mother, that thy father's heart was with
Her to the last.   Be true to her.   Honor
His love by loving for thyself and him.
And thou too, Gloster, look to her as now
I look to heaven.   A better friend will not
Be left behind.   And now the final wrench.
We have to part.   Farewell !   Heaven keep you as
The jewels of its crown !   [*Exeunt G., E., and Attenda*
   C.   A weary way !
But I am near my journey's end ; where is
My heart already, with the world behind.
Take ye the world—its pomps and vanities—
Who want !   I want it not.   What is it but
A bursting bubble of pretense, which, when
We trust it, vanishes ?   My portion is
Beyond the filching fingers of the years,
Well locked in the imperishable vaults
Of the eternal, where my kinghood has
Its highest royalties.   I would forget
The past—so dark with its ingratitudes
And crimes—in this the midnight of my wrongs.
These murderous rogues are bent upon my life.
   B. To think of them will only mar your peace ;
A thing half sacrilegious at the gate
Of heaven, where now you are.
   C.   Let Memory, then,
Evict them from her precincts, and my heart
Forgive the madness of their crimes.   Yea, let
Them take my life, if so the Giver wills.
I grudge Him not, since what He gave is His.
He pleased to give it, by myself unsought,
And holds me to account for proper use.
My trust concluded, He demands account.
Who knows what ills this early call escapes ?

The future—ah ! none penetrate its mists.
May He preserve the realm in spite of man,
Who madly throws the pilot overboard.

    B. The anchor of Heaven's purposes drags not ;
And let men drift, the shores of truth remain.
Your Majesty may comfortably rest
In thoughts like these, as on a bed of down,
And wait the sleep from which you wake with God.

    C. Most reverend lord ! My conscience and my God
Are all-sufficient comforters. The one
Acquits of ill ; the other gives all good.
Enough. I must prepare to close mine eyes.
Earth's twilight and heaven's dawn are kissing now.

                         [*Exeunt.*

ACT IV.

Scene I. *A coffee-house in London.*

    First Citizen. So pitiful it was, the way he died—
So like a king, while tender as a child ;
Composed and dignified, and nimbused with
Divinity, like mountain tops, at dawn,
Sheened with ethereal gold. He must have been,
By many mountain summits, nearer heaven
Than most men thought ; and, in exchanging worlds,
He had not far to fare.

    Second Cit.   Perhaps his heart
Contained the grace of royalty ; but there
It stayed, like a sequestered monk, who does
The world no good. Had all his life been as
His dying hour, his earlier deeds been as
His later state, posterity had known
Him as Saint Charles. Perchance Death rid
Him of the bad, and made the good seem as
A diamond found in mire.

First Cit.   Who knows but, had
We filled his place, we might have done his way?
Second Cit. Then had we both felt steel.
Third Cit.   You both had strode
The stage of life besmutted as the fiend
That rules the pit, and made your exeunt as
The saints of circumstance. A pity 'tis
That circumstances did not keep the king
A-dying all his life.
   First Cit.   Nay, give a dog
The credit of his decencies ; much more
A king.
   Third Cit. Credit for crouching when he feels
The whip ? Justice had caught the king, and Death
Was whipping him. This made his conscience whine,
And wrought in him politic penitence ;
A cat-o-nine-tails decency ; a shrewd
Commercial sanctity ; a gallows hope.
We need to thank the gentlemen who made
A saint of him and guarded 'gainst relapse.
   First Cit. Methinks that every life is but a rope,
Twisted by circumstances to its girth
And grain. Had we been kings, the texture of
Our minds, in all the convolutions of
Their thoughts, been formed like his, we should have
      been
His moral duplicates, twining, like vines,
Around the self-same ideal as our pole.
   Third Cit. Call thought, will, deed, the iron bands of
      our
Environment,which bind us slaves to Fate.
Then Fate, as master, will apply the lash.
Say one must murder—he must, therefore, lose
His head ; or sin, he must be damned. Causes
And consequences are but two in name,
Halves of one whole. But none are slaves except

As they enslave themselves. Though Charles could not
Be Arthur, Arthur Charles, each had a hand
In giving destiny a shape—master
Of circumstances this as that the slave ; -
And both by choice.
  First Cit.   True, Charles was free within
A circle of infirmity ; and yet
No less a slave, with a long chain at best.
  Third Cit. A slave to an infirmity of will,
When Truth and Right were knocking at his door ;
Yet strong enough to rise and bar them out.
Not negative infirmity his fault—
A conquered conscience and a tyrant will
Were the two gyves of Fate that held him fast.
Hence Arthur is embalmed while Charles will rot.
  First Cit. Have not so harsh a tongue to rasp a king
Whose tongue is still. Death has a mantle for
The faults of all.
  Third Cit.   Too scant to cover his.
Faults that are as dead leaves we brush away.
What stay, like festering thorns, after the bush
Is burnt, we execrate. He gave the pain
Of many punctures while he lived. Now the
Extracting of the thorns remains.
  Fourth Cit. [*Entering*].   The world
Is coming to an end.
  Third Cit.   'Twas ne'er so near.
  Fourth Cit. 'Tis horrible, past horrible ; yea, it
Is sacrilegious, laying murderous hands
Upon the sacred person of a king.
They amplified and magnified his faults.
His faults ? Heaven save me ! Who am I to say
His faults ? Or who are they, the Bedlam scum !
To judge a king of faults ? I disbelieve
The utmost syllable of what they charged
Whose daring did this diabolic deed.

None knows the end when such like deeds begin.
The throne is gone ; the church will go ; and then
The realm, the—everything will go ; and us
To boot.

   Third Cit. End thou thy speech ere ends the world.

   Fourth Cit. End or no end, but little boots us now,
When England comes to such an end as this.
My very marrow boils, as though a touch
Of judgment and of doom were in my bones,
As a presentiment of what awaits
This realm.

   Third Cit. Thou must be in a stew to have
Such fire about thy bones.

   Fourth Cit.   The world will feel
It ere an age be gone—to lose a king
In such a shameful way. I wonder that
The sun has heart to shine.

   Third Cit.   No doubt its heart
Is hot as thine. But oh, poor world ! that fails
For want of Charles's back to carry it.
What did the world before it had a Charles ?
So let it do now Charles is with the worms.

   Fourth Cit. He was a king—the very hand of God,
To execute His justice in the earth.

   Third Cit. No churl but matched the color of his blood.
His chin wagged like a beggar's when he ate.
The toothache wrung from him a vulgar groan.
The axe came down as on a Tyburn rogue.
But his divinity ! Whence got he that ?
From popish Mary's son ? or Noah's ark ?

   Fourth Cit. A *king.* There is 'twixt that and common
      words
A difference as between a million and
A millionth. But these desecrating knaves
Have wiped their feet on it, and cast it out
For every vagabond to trample on.

Power, God-invested, claims profound respect,
With worshipfulness in the supple knee.
But what presumption, madness, villainy,
Impiety, to touch its ark ! This tells
The tale why such unnumbered ills have seized
Us like the plague.
    Third Cit.   The greater power remains.
    Fourth Cit. It is satanic power.
    Third Cit.   Then Satan is
The greater power.
    Fourth Cit.   Nay, evil is allowed
To raise its head that Heaven may strike it off.
    Third Cit. So Charles raised his and it is gone.
    Fourth Cit.   Devil
Or man, thou hast the Devil's heart, to mock
The memory of a martyred king.
    Third Cit.   Then once
It was a great archangel's heart. Fie on
Thy flattery ! I am but a man. He thy
Great king was barely that, or he had still
Been king.
    Second Cit. 'Tis true, he had his faults.
    Fourth Cit.   Enough,
Perchance, to be a man. But he was king.
    Third Cit. Others there are who king the king ; hence
        must
Be more than king. Then reverence power in them.
    Fourth Cit. What ! Cromwell and the like ? the
        renegades
And regicides, with blood upon their hands !
Beshrew me if I come to that.
    Third Cit.   Forget
Not that a dead man's hand lacks gripe to save
Thee from the quick.
    Fourth Cit.   A dead king's memory may
Have potence that a living rebel lacks.

Third Cit. Belike, were Cromwell's heart the heart
       of Charles,
Thy tongue would reverence him with silence.   But
Great men endure what pigmies would resent.
Hence even calumny may vent itself
When greatness rules the honr.
     Fourth Cit.   Nay, say not force
Is greatness—brute, malignant force.   T'is but
The greatness of the ox that gores.
     Third Cit.   There is
More greatness in a Cromwell's finger than
The whole of Charles.
     Fourth Cit.   Heaven curse thee down from head
To foot, and shrive my soul for talking with thee !
               [*Rushing to the door he runs against a waiter
                     who has a cup of coffee*
Waiter. Zounds ! what were eyes intended for ?
Third Cit.   Pity
The blind who has king's-evil in his eye.
     Fourth Cit. Hang it ! That stain will never leave my
         doublet.
     W. And what of me, and all the coffee spilt ?
     Third Cit. That bodes ill luck to royalists. [*Exi
         Fourth Cit.*]   Look at
This Charles, who thought to be a doctor Faust,
To conjure with a crown.   In nature but
A porcupine, he rolled himself within
Himself and shewed the people but his quills.
His pseudo majesty of selfhood shut
Out love, except the love of self.   Admit
His friendship.   That he had—enough to use
A friend.
     Second Cit. Indeed, he used poor Strafford as
A staff, then cast him off.
     Third Cit.   A kingly deed—
The quintessence of Charles ! yet men adored

Him as a god enshrined in royalty.
But look at Cromwell, who has loomed up, like
A mountain from a fog, into the blue,
And overtops them all.   He mostly lives
Outside himself.   Hence his periphery
Of life has large circumference.   He has
The girth and stature of a man ; and when
He moves the foes of England quail.   I pin
No faith to men who always fail.   But those
Who touch the times with Midas-fingers, and
Transmute their gross events to gold, unlock
The temple gate of Fame and enter in.
    Second Cit. Think'st thou that Cromwell will be king?
    Third Cit.   Ay, king
Of men, by being kingliest of them all.
But whether king encrowned exceeds my reach.
Time tells his secrets when and how he will,
And we must wait the motions of his lips.   [*Exeunt.*

SCENE II. WHITELOCKE *and* WIDDRINGTON *meet in*
Hyde Park.

    Whitelocke. This day shews Nature in a gaudy trim,
With sky and earth as 'twere their bridal day.
Yet man is absonant and ill awry.
    Widdrington. Awry with discontent on every rung
Of life, if but because he fails to find
A cause for discontent.   Even a Charles,
Though tiptoed on the top, would still ascend,
Until he found the bottom, sans a head.
    Wh. He and the throne were woefully mismatched.
His littleness had much too large a place.
He was a penny in a puncheon ; and
Because he filled it with a noise, he thought,
Forsooth, that Charles could cram infinity.
What pity Cromwell lacks the royal blood !

He is a rainbow, shining brightest on
The blackest cloud, foretokening the calm.

Wid. We need at least a kingly substitute,
Who has the inward girth of royalty,
To fill the vacant palace of the king ;
For never exigence was great as this.

Wh. No cothurned pigmy will avail us now.
Our needs demand the stature of a man ;
And Cromwell is the manliest man we have.
Search England through we cannot find his match.
He is a king by the divinest right—
That of God-given ability to rule.
More kingly is he in exploits than king
Has been since famous Alfred's day.   Not that
It might be best to top him with the crown ;
For, were a subject kinged, the years might hatch
Us candidates for kinghood thick as flies.
Still, were he such, his actions would befit.

Wid. A paradox, my lord.   A king by right
Whom rightly we refuse.   Divinity
And policy at loggerheads.   The way
The times are, everything is paradox,
As though the realm were standing on its head.
Never, belike, was seen the like before.
Cromwell, you think, could set things on their feet.
Perhaps, if so he would.   But know you not
That wit and will are seldom on good terms ?

Wh. Methinks that Cromwell has both wit and will.

Wid. He has the wit to see what stroke to make ;
The nimbleness to strike when strokes will tell ;
But he has felt ambition, which can turn
The mightiest brain, and wreck the greatest soul.
Ambition is the offspring of the pit.
It obfuscates the mind, till selfishness
Puts on a cowl and hood, playing the monk,
And waxes fat by fasting in pretense.

It most deceives who think themselves sincere ;
For, thinking so, their conscience goes to sleep
And lets the passions dally with the will, ·
Which then becomes a blind impelling force,
Having no purpose save to spend itself.
That blindness was the hand of Fate to Charles.
Worse were the blindness with a greater force.

    Wh. I deem divine what makes a master man ;
And Cromwell, master of the masters, is
Divinest of divine among mankind.
But as he has, he still may serve the realm,
Unthroned. You charge him with ambition. 'Tis
Ambition rules the world ; and so he proves
His power to rule. Ambition's object gives
It character. If fair it be to judge
The object by the deed, his object is
To serve. England is what his hand has made her.
Scotland has felt his fist, Ireland his foot,
While England, like a mother, hangs upon
His arm. Hence his ambition wakes no fear ;

    Wid. The less we fear the more there is to fear ;
For our security supplies the door
Of entry to the most he may desire.
Who plans surprises tells not of his plans,
But lulls the watchers to security.
Go follow *Colonel* Cromwell, step by step,
Through all the winding paths of power, and see
How well he gave the opportunities
A turn, to gain this eminence. Admit
The pure integrity of his intent.
Now is a deeper impulse urging him,
With an intensifying eagerness,
To reach the throne. Ambition blindest is
With doubtful motives at its back, while yet
It wears the plume and breastplate of a good
Intent. Such blindness may be his. If his

It be, look out for Whitelocke ; look out all
Of us. Success, like scorpions, often kills
Who gave it birth. Act we the constable
And give this subject gyves, then question it.
Ask whether power to rule conveys the right.
If so, then Power were king ; and greater power
Would king both king and realm ; and greater still,
Grind us to dust. But here is not our sole
Alternative while royal stock abounds.

    Wh. Ah ! there it is you touch the solid ground.
A royal scion on the throne, to please
The superstitious craving of the realm,
With Cromwell as the sinew of the throne—
Its check and its support—our safety were
Assured.

    Wid.   We have the throne in hand ; so now,
The weaker king the easier to be held.
Here, then, our policy will be, to put
This greatest subject in the greatest place,
Subservient to the interests both of king
And us. So shall we stay the stomach of
Ambition with a compromise.

    Wh.   I fear
Me, Cromwell will not hear to it. Greatness
Is not entangled in a web of small
Contrivances.

    Wid.   The greatest elephant
Is none too great for man to take.

    Wh.   But here
We have an elephantine man, with head
To match his arm.

    Wid.   Our lead-and-line must sound
The depth of his designs.

    Wh.   So great a sea
Is fathomless.

    Wid.   Yet may we sound the shoals,

And estimate the nearness of the shore.

Wh. This meeting at the Speaker's may divulge
Beyond his forecast, should our ears be at
Their post, and wit perceive the kernel of
His words.

Wid. Step we upon his toes and, from
The way he ouches, learn his tender spot.   [*Exeunt.*

Scene III. Speaker Lenthall's. Members of Parliament *seated in the large hall.*

Speaker. (Addressing Cromwell.) This company, my
lord, in coming here,
Does homage to your will. The business you
Are ready to propound is urgent as
The steps of Time, which cannot brook delay.
This people has been favored of the Lord,
Who blessed the forces given you to command.
Allowing first our foes to shew their front,
He has rebuked them, giving you the skill,
And those you led the heart, to scatter them.
Now come the intricate necessities
Of peace, to bring from out the chaos of
Affairs the order on whose solid base
Prosperity and permanence must rest ;
To lay the corner-stone of which we need
To choose our future form of government.
Here is demanded—not the prowess of
The sword, but the achievements of the mind ;
And should we fail to seek some settlement
According to His will whose arm has led
Us hitherto, we shall be culpable,
And worthy of the vials of His wrath ;
Which may we, by our diligence, avert.

Harrison. The question that demands our thought is
this :

Having the power vouchsafed, what settlement
Can we devise, to make our civil and
Religious liberties secure to us
And permanent for our posterity ;
So that the mercies of the Lord may not
Be cast away, as if in thanklessness ?
With this great question we are eye to eye.

  Whitelocke. Great question ? Ay, and passing great ;
    nor one
To answer with a hasty tongue, but as
A problem of eternity. Yet here
Is the incarnate wisdom that has been
Our safety when the midnight gloomed. It were
A pity should it fail us now, in this
The noonday of success. It need not fail.
We want a settlement of our affairs
Upon a base abiding as the stars.
Then ask we of the settlement desired ;
Its form, and how to be secured. Shall we
Set up an absolute republic ? or
Prefer we somewhat of a monarchy ?

  Cromwell. His lordship has the question by the ear.
Let us not suffer it to slip our hold.
What shall we settle—a republic or
Mixed monarchy ? If aught monarchical,
In whom shall monarchy reside ?

  Widdrington to *Whitelocke* [*Aside*]. Now watch,
My lord.

  C.   'Tis ours, as sponsors for the realm,
To say.

  Wid. I think a monarchy, with due
Restraints upon its power, most in accord
With ancient English laws, and suitable
To meet the nation's needs ; and we must keep
As near the shore of ancient custom as
Will save us from the reefs, lest, venturing forth

On unknown seas, we lose ourselves. Hence I
Conclude it safe, and just, and wise, that, if
We choose the monarchy, we place the power
In one who represents his house who erst
Was king.

    Fleetwood. The question raised is greater than
The realm has tussled with this many an age ;
And 'twill not yield without a struggle as
Of life or death.

    St. John.   A settlement without
A monarchy—one that would leave our laws
Unshaken at the base, while robbing not
The people of their liberties—would tax
The tension of our wits to breaking point.
The genius of our government is such—
Our laws and methods are so grafted in
It—that to drop the monarchy, yet save
The constitution and the people's rights,
Would be to drop the heavens yet save the stars
From wreck. Our choice will put our future in
The mold.

    Sp.   Did we dispense with monarchy,
We would invite Confusion to control
Our destinies. These kingdoms know of naught
But monarchy ; nor care to know.

    Desborow.   What deep
Perversity of heart, what rheumy, dull
Stupidity of head, prevents in us
What others do, that we can not, like them,
Be constituted a republic and
Succeed ? Old England need not curtsey to
The best on earth. We have the wit ; we have
The decency ; we have the loyalty
To match the best. What need we more ?

    Wid. [*Aside.*]   See how
The lion whisks his tail.

D.   I trust her as
I would my mother's love.   Why may not all?
Wh. England is not the mushroom of a night.
Her institutions have been fed upon
The fat of time, deep in the subsoil of
The centuries, and may not be rudely torn
Away and leave her unimpaired.   Yea, and
The monarchy is such a vital part—
The very tap-root of the government—
That its excision so would dislocate
The forms and processes of law, the courts
Would be reduced to bedlam, anarchy ;
And twenty lifetimes might not see the end.

Whalley. I own myself unskilled in matters of
The law.   I know not all the labyrinths
In which bewildered clients lose their all.
I am not versed in technicalities
That give to deeds the color of one's gold.
It baffles me to fathom why we need
This costly tinsel glittering on a throne.
And baffled were we all, I ween, if asked
The why.   But if we be so much bewitched
That king there must be, whom have we to choose ?
The king's first son is reddened with our blood.
The next, in heart, is redder than our blood.

Wid. The Duke of Gloster still is in our midst,
And yet too young to have the virus of
Our enemies within his veins.   Docile
And ductile in the uncorruption of
His boyhood, we may mold his mind to fit
The office so that it will fit the realm.

Wh. A day might be in which the eldest son—
Or in his lieu the Duke of York—might come
Before the parliament and bind himself
By such conditions and restraints as would
Insure the realm against his prejudice,

And make innocuous all his present spleen.
Misfortune, when it feels its utterness,
Will lick the hand that laid its pride in dust.
    C. Such answers answer not the question asked—
Suggest not *somewhat* of a monarchy,
But recommend the resurrection of
The king, rancored and raging in the son
For red revenge. Bind him with contracts is
Proposed—with laws—with breath—with pen-and-ink.
Bind the north wind with spider webs ! Then may
You bind a Stuart with devices that
Would hold a man. 'Twere but to try, with odds
Against success, what failed before. Think not
That you will ever read his heart, or eye,
Or lip. They are but convex mirrors that
Deceive the eye. Think not experience will
Be eyesalve to his youth. A Stuart learns
But to improve on craft with deeper craft,
And how to grease a lie with greater show
Of guilelessness.
    Wid.   That theme inspires his tongue
To fluency. [*To Wh., aside.*]
    C.   And yet the fact remains :
We need a settlement. We cannot drift
Without a helmsman on the open seas
And shun the rocks. The best-manned ship is oft
In straits to make her port. If safely, and
With preservation of our rights as men
And Christians, we can make a settlement,
With monarchy enough to give a head,
It will effectually secure our weal.
But we have held that we must have a king,
And he of some specific lump of clay,
As the sole stuff with kingly attributes.
I stigmatize the thought. We need a man,
Brought for his fitness from the common lump.

Take ye your thingling made of precious dirt ;
Approach it as an august mightiness ;
Address it as a god in miniature :
Soon we have more than human—as a fool.
Repeat the sire's undoing in the son :
We magnify the follies of the sire
And make one fit to be the king of fools.
This we have done until the arrogance
Of imbecility o'erstomachs us.
Now wisdom whispers in our ear to seek
A man, whose heart, and head, and arm, the Lord
Has formed to finish what is well begun.
Necessity is asking for the man.
God give us eyes to see the man we need !

    Wh. That has a smack of reason after all.   [*Aside.*

    Wid. If but an honest heart be at its back. [*Exeunt.*

SCENE IV. *In the park of* Speaker LENTHALL. CROM-
WELL *and* HARRISON *sauntering.*

   Cromwell. I know not where is Babel worse than that
We leave. I put a question. All grew big
With pomp of fluency, and, laboring hard,
Brought forth—a belch of wind. What heads to do
The thinking for a realm ! Some think that time
Is but a moping owl, blinking among
The ivied ruins of the past, screeching
The night away ; whereas it heralds us
The dawn that bids awake. Others would use
Proleptic haste, and make the sun rise from
A mangonel, to reach Utopia at
A bound. Familiar things grow frightful in
A fog—since clothed in the surrounding garb
Of dreariness—and lose proportion both
In size and shape. Hence these, beholding through
A mental fog, see not the outlines of

Affairs. Hence are their trembling wits afraid
To act : bar those who shut their eyes
To leap, e'en should it be to doom. 'Tis now,
As never since this bloody strife began,
We need a falcon's eye to see our need,
And then a falcon's wing to make the stoop.
Instead, are fiddle-faddle, scamble, and
A malt-horse going round and round to nowhere.

Harrison. The parliament might be aroused to shew
The gristle of a sturdy will, and to
Outstep the shadow of its former self.
Numbers, we know, give confidence to act.

C. The parliament has found Cockaigne, in which
It lolls in drowsy listlessness, deeming
The years a well-aired bed of down, duties,
Lethean essences of flowers, to make
Voluptuous its repose. Its energy
Is but a windmill of garrulity.
The fact is, Major, that the parliament
Is but a hydra-headed Charles. It does
Not represent these kingdoms, but itself ;
And like its prototype, it wields the powers
Of government against the general will ;
While plotting to perpetuate itself,
Either to eternize its tyranny
Or smuggle to the throne the spawn of him
We spurned.

H.   Think you so much as that ?
C.   If deeds
Have tongues their deeds say that ; which fact brings
      fear
Lest patience has a faultiness, in thus
Enduring what we might prevent.
H.   Nay, have
We power to match the will, and will to meet
The muscle of so great emergency ?

C. The Lord is match for all emergencies.
His right hand drew me from obscurity,
And placed me on an eminence of power,
Whence I could view the dangers, woes, and wants
Of this distracted realm, and urged me on
To deeds that were its medicine. The last
Obstruction to a cure remains : and worst
As well as last. He still is urging me
To use a thorough remedy. I shrink,
Like Moses, yet, like him, am driven before
This inward word of power, which bids me fare.
To act, I brave the parliament ; while not
To act, I brave the Lord : and verily,
Omnipotence is hard to brave ; but, at
My back, He gives omnipotence. I must—
Unless the parliament awake—I must
Proceed.

    H.   Still to deplete the house ?

    C.   Ay, to
Dissolve it, and to send the sluggards to
Their homes, to drowse their lives away.

    H.   Dissolve,
My lord ! A daring thing were that. Then must
You wink at precedent and set the world
Agog.

    C.   These precedents are quivers, whence
The tyrant draws the arrows of oppression.
I heed them not. To-day is master of
To-day, not a galled slave that cringes at
The heels of yesterday, nor tyrant of
To-morrow. Every day has weather of
Its own. Hence yesterday's great-coat serves not
The sunshine of to-day. The Lord is not
Enmeshed with precedents. He turns
Not round to search behind for copies from
The past, but moves right on. So must we do ;

Nor halt for mountains lying in our course,
Because we crossed them not before ; but on,
Up, towards the height of glory that awaits
Mankind.

    II.   If only we could read His will—
An open book.

    C   Who, with His word in hand,
His Spirit in the heart, wills well to do
His will, is guided by the truest light,
And shall not greatly err. I have that light ;
And in the most divine recess of soul,
Behind the arras of my grosser self,
A still-voiced mentor says : " Walk in the light."

                                 [*Exeunt.*

SCENE *V.* *House of Commons.* CROMWELL *beckons*
   HARRISON, *who approaches and turns his ear.*

    Cromwell [*Whispering*]. The time to act is come, and
       act I must
As I would give account. Be firm.
    Speaker.   Are you
Ready for the question ?
    Several members.   Ready. Question.
Put it to the vote. Ready. Vote.
    C. [*Rising, hat in hand*].   My voice
Has not been heard ; nor had it been had not
Occasion forced me into speech. Believe
Me, what I say shall be from honest heart,
And honestest of all its honesties.
The parliament of which you are both part
And an addendum, will, in history, seem
The ocean-rock on which a despot king
Has hurled his billows, to behold them crush
And crumble into futile foam. It has
Withstood the flabby doubts and craven fears
Which took the spirit out of weaker men

eft the coward warden of their hearts.
uld not breathe the faintest breath of blight
on a single leaf of amaranth
.hat it has won. And yet, I have a word
Of truth, which, woe is me, as I regard
This realm and Him who summoned me to its
Relief, if I withhold. The scars of great
Injustices are on the army's heart,
Whose blood was given for you, for me, for all.
The land is in a mournful mood, because
Your leafy promises of amnesty
Were hollow at the heart. For life is nought
When you have robbed men of the means of life.
Those who, amid life's peltings of mishap,
Were overwhelmed, have found a dungeon doom.
And there you let them languish year by year.
Two years have you, with ponderous arguments,
Been laboring at the laws, to shew results
That call for spectacles. The want of wants
Is, godly ministers to break the bread
Of life. But ye have left the souls of men
To starve. And now at last, to magnify
Your selfishness, to monarchize yourselves
On a perpetual whirligig of power—

Wentworth. This is strange language, Mr. Speaker, I
Protest ; such language as a parliament
Was never called till now to hear ; and this
From one, our servant, whom we trusted in
Good faith ; on whom our lavish honors have
Descended with the frequency of dew,
And the full copiousness of April showers ;
One whom—

C.   Come, come ! enough of this. [*Putting on
his hat and stepping forth.*] 'Tis time
These pratings had an end ; whose emptiness,
For several mortal years, has soughed between

These walls like wind-ghosts in the woods. I will
No more. The army will no more; the realm
No more. Nay, God himself is weary of
Your words. Such cumberers of the ground, in this
The garden of the Lord, must come out by
The roots. Ye must. Ay, *must*, and shall ! It is
Unfit that ye should stay and keep the blush
On England's cheek, the fire within her heart.
Already you have been too long for aught
That you have done that were a credit to
The footmen at your heels. You now shall give
A place to better men ; to men who have
The nation in their heart, instead of self ;
Men who believe in God, instead of craft ;
Men who are armor-bearers for the truth ;
Yea, champions of the laws ; yea, heroes of
Humanity. Call them in. Call them in. [*To Harrison.*
           Enter Musketeers.
You call yourselves a parliament. You are
No parliament. I tell you that you are
No parliament. You are but clingers to
The coat-tail of a parliament. You do
No more than represent yourselves. You are
Not wanted by the nation, as you know.
Hence have you made a sneak-hole for yourselves,
Through which to creep and be a parliament.
Some of you are drunkards—walking barrels,
Full of yeasty wind, which makes your tongues wag.
Some live in stark contempt of God's commands.
Slaves to your greedy appetites—you do
Your duty by the Devil's decalogue.
No wonder you are deaf when godly men
Cry out for ministers. Some are corrupt
In heart, unjust indeed ; a scandal to
The gospel ye pretend a reverence for.
You cannot be a parliament for those

Who honor God.   You cannot make just laws
Who are yourselves unjust.   Depart, I say,
And let us see no more of you ; and so
Do one good deed before you die.   Ay, go
Ye ; in the Lord's name, go ! [*He seizes the mace.*]
   What shall be done
With this vain bauble ?   Take it off.   [*Handing it to a
   musketeer.*]   Now bring
Him down. [*Pointing to the speaker.   Harrison ap-
             proaches.*
 Speaker.   Nought less than force can make me move.
 H. Then I will lend a hand to serve your turn.
  [*The Speaker descends and members begin to retire.*
 C. 'Tis you yourselves who have constrained to this.
My soul has wrestled night and day, as in
Gethsemane, to find escape.   But God
Has grown so weary of your ways, that this
Alone would serve His will ; and I submit.
Your insolencies to his Majesty
Could be no more endured ; so justice comes.
        [*To Sir H. Vane.*
O thou, Sir Harry Vane ! Sir Harry Vane !
Thou hast belied thy possibilities,
And done thyself, thy country and thy God,
Immeasurable wrong.   Hadst thou not given
Thy mind a prey to casuistries, and let
Thy tongue perform the great old serpent's part,
Thou mightest have prevented this.   One flash
Of lightning honesty from out the sky
Of an exalted soul, had shivered all
Their sophistries and cleared the atmosphere.
But thou hast been a recreant to thy trust.
Go then, thou spendthrift of thy morning hours,
And put life's afternoon to penitence.
Go all of you, and think upon your ways.
Reflect, that God gave once a golden bowl,

Brimmed with His foaming opportunities ;
But you have let it slip your grasp into   .
The depths of the unfathomable years.
The Lord deliver me from Harry Vane !
The Lord deliver me from all of you !   [*Exeunt.*

SCENE VI.   *Chancery   Court,   Westminster   Hall.*
Judges, Lord Mayors *and others.* CROMWELL, in *a
black velvet suit, seated in the chair of state.*
Commissioners *approach,* LAMBERT *bearing the civil sword.*

Lambert. Your highness need not be reminded what
Distractions have beset this realm, like beasts
Of prey, these many years.   Nor need I give
To these the judges, mayors and gentlemen,
Enumeration of your services.
In those we hear a loud demand for one
To head the realm ; while these respond that you
Are tried and proven capable.   Here then,
As mouthpiece for this triple commonwealth,
I do beseech you, as myself her friend,
And you the doughtiest, ablest of her sons,
To give yourself unto the office of
Protector, and assume the duties that
Devolve therewith ; in doing which, you will
Complete the blessing of your services,
Which have enriched her when she else were poor.
In this I ask for her the favor, and
Of you the sacrifice, that is its price.
   Cromwell. As in the sight of God, I do confess
Myself as having seen the drift of the
Events that culminate to-day, and here :
As who did not whose eyes could look right on ?
Not that I tried to form a channel for
Them ; but I found myself upon a stream,

Whose current bore me in resistless arms,
As at the mandate of Omnipotence.
As God has seen my heart, He knows that I
Have had no mind to this, except as I
Have yielded to His will, as plainly seen.
If erred I have, it was in striving to
Avoid the bourn to which His hand would lead.
It were superfluous to enumerate
The perfidies and despotisms of
The king, whose retributions ended his
Career, or to expatiate on the course
Of dilatoriness, obtuse neglect
Of duty, and unseemly eagerness
To oligarchize, with a semblance of
Legality, of those the residue
Of what was once a parliament.
You saw in what predicament I found
The realm, and how I had to bring it thence.
When forced to take the helm of power, I called
Together such of godly sort as held
The best credentials for their wit, in hope
That they might overhaul the tackle of
The State, making her trim, and, through the church,
Give ballast in a better ministry.
These, taking soundings, came to shoals, in which
Were numberless impediments, and such
Anfractuosities of stream as mocked
Their ingenuity. And now, in sheer
Despair, they turn, as to a pilot, thus
To me. I know not why, save that the Lord
Has heretofore vouchsafed to use me as
His Moses, to conduct His people through
War's wide red sea. In this their confidence,
And in His long-continued mercies, and,
Moreover, in the indications of
His will, I read my new commission, which

Enlarges my responsibilities ;
And this so much it makes my duties more
Than those that were too great for them. I will
Not say the office is superfluous ; for
We need a center of authority,
A rallying point of power, in which, as 'twere,
To individualize the prowess of
The realm ; a something that shall have the good
Of monarchy without the ill ; in which
Constabulary Duties shall not threat
The people with the gyves of tyranny.
This office, and these duties, you invite
Me to assume ; to which your will I give
My full consent. And may His hand, which in
The past has kept, now keep me faithful to
The higher trust.

    Lambert [*Cromwell standing*]. Your highness, having
      learned
The form of government provided, and
Become familiar with the same, do now
Assent thereto in all and every of
Its articles, and swear, in presence of
Almighty God and these assembled, to
Observe, and keep, and execute the same,
So help you God ?

    C.   I do.

    L. [*Kneeling*].   This sword I give
Your highness, as a symbol of the power
Invested by the realm in you as its
Executive. The scabbard holds it, as
A sign of power in peace. It can be drawn.
This tells that Justice must not fail to smite
When danger threats, or smite until it threats.

    C. I take it and return my own [*Exchanging*], in
      sign
That I shall rule by law and not by force.

My own I give you sheathed, in token that
Its mission is fulfilled.   There may it sleep !
And now a word about the voyage on
The unknown sea whose breakers fall upon
The beaches of eternity.   With sky
Above and dim expanse before, I spread
My sails, with trust in Him who made both sky,
And sea, and all that is.   In doing right—
As right I mean to do, and only right—
I shall not do as every man deems right.
For as I trust the wisdom from above,
So I expect it will not well agree
With that below.   But as the captain heeds
His compass, not his passengers, so I
Shall heed the compass in my breast, whose pole
Is the Eternal Throne.   For, verily,
The rocks that push their jagged shoulders from
The deep, need more than human vigilance
And wit to clear.   I see the fragments of
Malignancy, in pirate factions, with
An eye from out their shelter, watching for
A chance to bear down, unawares, upon us.
I see the levelers, who would o'erwhelm
The social decencies of life, bring down
A waterspout of ruin on the state,
And wreck the church with idiot liberties.
I see the mental debauchees who prate
Of conscience when they mean the freedom of
The pit ; who fain would loose the helm, and have
None feel restraint, but drift unmoored.   I see
The catharists ensurpliced in pretense,
Subverting order, bidding us renounce
The laws and let our sails, in savage winds,
Flap into tatters, hoping He whose voice
Once lullabied the sea will speak and save.
I see the Roman rats of Jesuitry—

Insensible of aught save hunger's pangs—
With teeth of craft, eating great holes into
The bottom of the ship. All these I see.
But who shall pierce, with a prophetic eye,
The mist and spray of policies that hang
Between ourselves and other nations ; though
We hear the rotings of the surge ? Never
Before has people been in such a plight ;
And never ruler placed in such a strait.
But never was a struggle for so much.
And not before has nation done so much
To show the world the way to liberty.
Our courage, and withal the crown of our
Success, will speak in thunder in the ear
Of Tyranny, Beware ! while every age
Will be the stronger for our deeds ; and this
As they are done in the Almighty strength.
For this I pray. On this may all rely.   [*Exeunt.*

ACT V.

Scene I. *A parlor of a palace. Isle of Jersey.*

Hyde. There have been whispered divers pregnant
    hints
Of means that circumstances justify,
By which your Majesty may be possessed
Of all your patrimony at a stroke.
    Charles. Why hints, which are but wind, instead of
    deeds ?
    H. They may be shadows of approaching deeds,
Or the prophetic guaranty of deeds,
Or the green lobes of germinating deeds.
    C. Good luck assist their wits ! That brings to mind
The singing of a bird beside the door,
But yesterday. Its limpid note had such

A gush of sweetness as the brooks in spring
Have, when they babble by the peppermint.
I vow, it trickled through my very soul.
Suppose you, Hyde, insensate things possess
Symbolic qualities, which only need
Interpreting to find their correlates
In other things?

     H.   That were in consonance
With nature's unities.

     C.   Then why may not
Events concatenate, and that which is
Be a prophetic clew to what will be?

     H. I see no place for negative to that.
One human pair, and countless pairs result.
One sun, and days are but the opening of
His eyes. One rain, and every daisy laughs.
One bird-song, and a prince is glad. Could we
But hear the song, and know what ears would hear,
And have our fingers on the nerves behind
The ears, and know how many other hearts
Would catch the glad contagion of the first,
And others that of these,—a thrush's note
Might change the moods and motions of a realm
And shape its destiny, and, through it, change
The world. So latent possibilities
Are pent in everything, and but await
The fiat of a fitting circumstance
To bring them out. So are there elements
Of prophecy in everything. Had we
The alphabet we soon might read the page.

     C. That fancy flickered in my mind as light
That dances from a mirror on the wall.
Fancy, I said ; but that may not be all.
Our fancies often are the soul of facts.
That bird—who knows how much its note implied ?
Its song upon a rainy day—how apt

As a precursor of the hope you give !
Besides, my right palm itched persistently
An hour ago ; a sign that I shall get
A something that will please.   Thus prophecy
On prophecy, in enigmatic form,
Precedes the bruiting of your tidings.   But
The means.   I wish you had not said, By means
That circumstances justify ; as though
The circumstances would not justify
Whatever means it pleases me to use.
Shall Heaven's anointed son of saintly sire
Sit on the loathsome dunghill of his wrongs,
And haggle with philosophers about
The righteousness of means to gain his rights?
H. The means are lightning yet imprisoned in
The clouds.   I cannot tell you, save that they
Will strike your greatest foe.
   C.   The gods pour down
A honeydew of luck on that !
   H.   The means are such
That Cromwell's person would not miss their aim.
   C. Heaven grant the lightning may descend and burn
The bloodstain from his guilty hand.
If life should pay for life, then let him pay ;
And cursed be Pity if she shed a tear !
H. Here Policy to Circumspection holds
Her ear attent.
   C.   What, grandam Policy
Uplift her birch to tame a king, and he,
In Circumspection's fool's-cap, take a stool ?
Politic as to means of thwarting wrong,
And circumspect in giving regicides
Their dues?   Does Hyde, of all I trust, say that ?
Justice, sir, is true policy ; and were
My hands but circumspectly round their necks,
My wish would be for fifty more to squeeze.

A martyred father's blood is crying from
The ground ; and Heaven refuse to shrive me if
My ear grows deaf.
  H.   Your Majesty has missed
The bull's-eye of my thought. We have to fence
With circumstances ; hence must guard as well
As thrust. All feel a shrinkage at the heart
At thought of taking off a wearer of
God's image, though defaced. Hence were it well
To keep your hand unstained.
  C.   God's image ! Say
Beelzebub's.
  H.   I say not, Spare the deed
On one whose soul is black with guiltier deed,
But spare yourself.
  C.   Myself indeed ! A fig
For shivering qualms and womanish conceits,
When Retribution stands beside the grave
Of martyred Innocence and calls for blood !
That is no time for Conscience to be pert.
Beshrew me, Hyde ! could we but vivisect
The soul, we might discover that this thing
We call a conscience oft is cowardice.
Our very nature is a hypocrite.
We have an ague of the heart and call
It conscience, to conceal timidity.
Now if, by sparing of myself, you mean
The putting of my heart in swaddling-clothes,
I tell you in the bravest English, I
Prefer to be a man. I shall not quail
For all the ghosts that ever flitted through
The chambers of the night.
  H.   Prudence has heart,
And courage is not blind. Bethink, and ask
Yourself, Should Europe know that England's king
Had turned avenger in the dark—though just

The deed as plunge of Lucifer from heaven—
What fumigation could deodorize
Your royal robes of the assassin's taint?
Were Cromwell in your hands, you would not fill
Jack's place and ply the axe.

    C.   The dark! I am
Already in the dark. What is behind
The *whereas* of this long preamble?

    H.   This:
A plan has found inception in the heart
Of loyalty, to give the lofty lord
A lasting quietus.

    C.   Amen! And may
The Devil take his soul, lest he should mar
My sainted father's peace.

    H.   In such a way
That, while you figurehead it with your name,
You may remain in ignorance of the
Minutiæ of the plan, and so, in truth,
Be able to conceal yourself within
The shadow of your ignorance.

    C.   Proceed.
There is a smack of something there.

    H.   Suppose
Experts in wit and skill should be assured
A given sum, with which to serve your cause,
And he who serves you best receive, besides,
Emoluments for life.

    C.   And that he should,
Without a grudge or stint.

    H.   No service could
Be greater than to clear a passage to
The throne.

    C.   In that were everything.

    H.   You need
Not know the how of it or father what

Is done.

C.   A glass of wine.   Claret, to clear
My wits. [*Served by page.*] I like the thought.   Yes, by
         the meek
And martyred innocence of him whose name
I bear, I like the thought.   It takes the cork
From out my heart and makes me sparkle as
The wine.   You would provide a paradise
Of ignorance, to save my innocence,
Or furnish fig-leaves in extremity.
A loyal thought !   Well, blab what may be blabbed.

H. You let my head and hand be proxy for
Your own, in making out a document
As hinted at ; whose contents will be yours
No more than Adam's epitaph.

C.   And in
The document let hints be broad enough
To bid defiance to the rest of speech
To overlap.

H.   They shall be understood.
The object gained, you may, as honestly
As innocence at prayers, keep open face,
Rebutting all the censures of the world,
By disavowal of the document.

C. The Devil will be counterwitted there.
Yet why should any censure, disapprove,
Demur ?   Bring all the world to Jersey isle,
To duplicate my lot—it would revise
Its sentiments.   But what it is it is.

H. Only my loyalty, and zeal to serve
Your Majesty, could make me so far strain
My scruples.   But the circumstances give
Their sanction to unordinary means.

C. There now !   No need to be so smock-faced, Hyde.
This hide-and-seek with Conscience is a game
For children, women and the dying, in

Progressive mode—good, better, best. So Hyde
Would hide and let his Conscience seek.   Who would
Be bad when goodness is so cheap ?   Ah well !
A little Conscience, now and then, will keep
Our souls in trim for whatsoe'er may hap—
That is, a reasonable Conscience ; but
If Conscience plays the prude, outstare her with
An eagle eye, and go as Duty bids.
That is philosophy ; and good enough
To be a parson's text.   What need we more ?
We have the sanctions of a righteous cause,
With every motive in a priestly frock.
But have you inklings who has loyalty,
And wit, and nerve, to serve this turn ?
 H.   I have
Been urged by divers men of consequence
To set your Majesty on this, assured
That they would find the fitting instruments.
 C. Why, said you not that you had only hints ?
 H. I said that I had hints, which word is true.
In having more, my word is more than true.
But true it is I have not all the truth.
The how and what of means is not disclosed,
But waits your royal word.
 C.   Then use my name
As best may serve its owner's purposes.
I will not curse the horse that takes me home.
             [*Exeunt.*

Scene II. *A dimly lighted room in London.*

 Fox. See that the guard is at his post ; for not
A keyhole must be left unwatched, lest some
Obtrusive ear frustrate our plans.
 Gerard [*opening the door and looking*]. All right.
 F. Wary to plan and bold to execute.

That motto guarantees success.   E'en now
Events are brightening, as the realm awakes
To loyalty, and all converge in rays
Of promise on our sacred sovereign's crown.
While we unite the enemy divides ;
Which fact is double pledge of good.   The mad
Fanatics have the army in ferment ;
While parliament provokes their testy ire,
By dawdling indolence ; in which it proves
How much these kingdoms need a lawful head.
Alured in the dumps, with others of
His kind, and Overton concocting means
Of playing second Oliver, will draw
Attention from ourselves ; while, underground,
We charge the mine whose one explosion will
Exalt the traitors to the clouds [*Laughter*].   Meanwhile,
The parliament and he we think of most,
Are dancing different jigs.

    G.   The devil keep
Them dancing while we work.

    Henshaw.   Ludlow is said
To champ his bit.

    F.   They are in somersault,
The head and feet reversed, and all rolled up
In indistinguishable jumbledness ;
Which is a thing of course.   How can a watch
Keep time with mainspring gone ?

    Vowell.   Ludlow at outs
Will give to Rupert open door to get
The Irish armed.

    F.   Rupert to Rupert's work,
And we to ours.

    V.   And yet we scan the sky
Ere leaving home without umbrella.

    F.   We
May look on these propitious auguries

With gladsome eyes.   But not our eyes, our hands
Are in demand.   The arch usurper sits
And sucks the sweets of his security.
But our anointed sovereign suffers in
The ashes of his woe ; while we are wheels,
Whose turning on the axle of the times
Must bear things on, or, by our tardiness,
Give Treason breathing time.   Then turn we to
Our hearts, and let us ask them whether they
Are ready for the loyalest of deeds ;
And as they are, so let us do.
    G.   Why should
Our arm lack length to reach the throne and rid
Us of our incubus ?
    F.   Bravo !   Gristle
And soul are at the back of that.   The heart
Of Gerard finds his tongue, without a touch
Of hat to Cowardice.   The man was in
The heart ; but now, the heart is in the man.
    V. Our breath is but a zephyr till we act,
Laden with drowsy perfumes of desire.
Action will be a gusty force, which beats
The bald scalp of the mountain till it moans.
Hope in our heart, our help is in our hand ;
Hope to inspire to deeds, the deeds to save.
There is our glittering cynosure.   Yet cast
We not ourselves on war's contingencies,
To reel in bloody havoc at the best.
We must be economical of blood,
And carry certainty in one firm hand ;
Which is the wiser, braver policy.
Wiser, since done as well, and cheaper done ;
Braver, since little dares and does so much.
    Finch. I challenge bravery that would take a life
By theft, and honor done the king by a
Dark-corner deed.   The king is owner of

The throne, whose allocated benefits
Are ours.   Then let our courage boldly wrench
These kingdoms from his grasp who holds them in
Unrighteousness.   There is a kingliness
Becoming kings, which gives its flavor to
Their deeds ; a dignity that raises them
To stateliness above the petty ways
Of common men : an attribute that we
Must honor by our deeds.
    G.   He serves his king
The best whose deeds accomplish most.
    F.   His deeds
Do most who saves the honor of the king ;
For, void of that, how paltry is a throne !
A monarch's honor is his diadem.
His throne and honor make him all a king.
    G. Remember Naseby, and beware lest we
Should leave him neither honor nor a throne.
Treason that has an army at its back,
Can more than match our unarmed loyalty.
    H. We see no serpent in the royal arms,
But rampant Lion-and-the-unicorn.
Cannot we fit our forces for a leap ?
    F. Force has been wasted till we need to spare.
The time has come for individual deeds.
Gerard and Vowell are the stuff that dares ;
And daring is the measure of a soul.
There is a grandeur in its deeds which gives
A kinghood second only to the king's.
And now the tonic of the times must make
Us hungry for distinction.   [*A noise outside the door.*]
        What is that ?
Sh—list !   [*The door opens.*]   Why, Billingsley ! you
        gave one's hair
A quickening at the roots.
    Billingsley.   I had so good

A bruit I had scant patience with the guard.

F. Which proves that he was not in duty scant.

B. Tidings, like liquor, when a man is full,
Derange his thinking gear.

      G.   And good thou say'st?

B. The best of many a day—enough to make
Despair look up and laugh.

      G.   God speed thy tongue,
And blessings on thy soul!

      B.   'Twas smuggled o'er
The sea. I read the paper for myself—
A noble document! proceeding from
The king.

      V.   Then royal.

      B.   Royal as the king,
Being the reflex of his royal mind.

G. Out with it, man!

      B.   His Majesty has sent
A proclamation, big with promises
To those his loyal subjects who shall give
Him one triumphant deed of service.

      G.   One!
My arm is ready for a score, if such
He needs. But the particulars.

      B.   He rails
On Cromwell as a base mechanic knave;
A traitor villain from the gutter spewed
And spilled upon the throne : and that he is.
He piously beseeches us to rid
The earth of this unchristian rogue, and do
Ourselves and him a worthy turn; for which
He promises to who will poison, stab,
Shoot, or otherwise destroy the traitor,
Knighthood and five hundred pounds a year; ay,
Employment, too, so long as he shall live.

      V. A kingly offer for a knightly deed.

F. Beyond a peradventure know you this ?

B. The language was too kingly in the pomp
And stateliness of its array for less
Than king.

    G.   Assuredly.   His Majesty
Has shewn a Christian patience to endure
So long the insolence of this low dog,
Who makes the throne a kennel. But at last
His justice lifts its glittering axe. In this
We see the sterner aspect of the king's
Divinity. Now for responding to
His righteous will, with plan well aimed and sure
To reach its mark.

    V.   His Majesty divines
The secrets of the hour, with prescience born
Of royalty, and sees in this the time
To strike the shackles from the land. We then,
As loyal subjects, *must* respond.

    B.   And then
The guerdon when the work is done !

    Finch.   As bids
The king 'tis ours to do, e'en though it were
To tread the tempest-shredded waves. He has
His reasons that we know not of, which, did
We know, would, doubtless, thrill our hearts as when
A clarion splits the morning air.

    H.   There is
A smack of bravery in his words, which come
From him as cloudy messengers, and tell
Of arming thunderbolts behind. I ween
The French and Irish are in leash, ready
To cast and bring the quarry from the height
Of its security. For, Cromwell gone,
The governmental bastardy will end,
When these have stooped.

    F.   We are agreed ;

And so we have a pledge of luck.   Who will
Be father of a plan to serve the king?
  G. Recall we that the kingdoms are at stake ;
A stake for which we all shall risk our all.
Our *all*—our names, our fortunes and our lives,
And smut the dearest that we leave behind.
In such a game it will not do to drowse.
Our hearts must have a stout heroic beat ;
Our thews be stiff as iron under strain ;
Our minds be clear as sunshine after shower ;
Our purpose changeless as the mind of God.
Fail we in one of these, we fail in all ;
And that would be old England's day of doom.
Roused by such thoughts, let none of us dare drowse.
Then what do we devise ?   But first, what force
Have we that may be trusted as ourselves ?
I give my word for twenty-five, who will
Not turn their backs when danger threats.
  F.   They need
To know the knack how not to use their tongues,
And when, and where, and how to show their face.
  G. They may be trusted as the fingers on
My hands.
  H.   Add five as trusty as the best.
  V. My men are in myself, who will not fail.
  G. Thirty.   A decent force for decent deeds.
  V. Decent enough to warrant something bold,
By which the traitor may be taken by
Surprise ; for he would fear a rabbit's bite
Ere boldness on our part, who seem so tame.
Heaven knows we have been tame enough.   But tush !
Why cry o'er last year's toothache when the king
Invites us to a feast?
  F.   A plan.   We want
A loyal plan to serve a royal cause.
  V. Your nose, I see, is keen upon the scent.

F. Ay, Fox my name, the fox is in my nose.
And now, so near the poultry-yard, we need
To be awake. A plan. Propound a plan.
Who will be Fortune's valet for the nonce?

V. I have it to an ace. On Saturdays
My Lord Protector rides to Hampton Court,
Giving an opportunity than which
The mills of Fortune could not better make.

Finch. A very godsend of a thought.

H.   'Twill give
A smack of daring to the deed to do
It in the open eye of day ; and that
Is what we need to save the honor of
The king.

G.   I care not e'en the twirling of
A straw about the means so we but gain
The end ; for any stick were clean enough
To crack the skull of this malfeasant knave,
Or poison good enough that would but eat
The core and essence of his life. But here
We have a cue to that which cannot fail.
Our project has two aspects. How shall we
Employ our force ? How frustrate his ?

Finch.   We might,
To-morrow, meet him midway in the road,
And part to let him pass, then close and make
Assault, shooting the dog to death. That done,
Outspeed the news to London and proclaim
The king.

B.   With one to aid, I will secure
The horses of his troopers as they graze
At Islington, and baffle all attempts
At hasty meddling with our plans.

H.   There are
The soldiers at the mews, who must be seized,
Unarmed, and made secure.

F.   I will assist
In making all secure.

V.   I cannot shoot,
Hence cannot make assault. But Billingsley
Shall have my hand ; the work my head ; the king
My heart. I see high promise in our plan,
In which our personal diversities
But help to unify, according to
The analogues in nature's alchemy.
Monotony in hue, tone, form, offends
The sense. Contrasts beget comparisons
And give the mind a healthy exercise.
Hence beauty has variety and gives
Exhilaration to the soul ; and this
Variety is basic unity.

F. That smells of desks and musty books. But deeds
We need, not desks ; and blows, not books.

V.   True words
Are heralds of true deeds.

F.   The hour asks words
With ring of steel and fire of flint, and deeds
Whose motions have the lightning's wing and are
As daring as the pirate infidels
Of Barbary. These we can give who have
So good a cause. But pardon me the haste
Of an impetuous tongue. I know your heart
Is loyal as the Union Jack.

V.   Ay, that
It is.

G.   Now for the kingdoms for the king,
And honor for ourselves till time shall end.
To-morrow meet we, in the slaty dawn,
Here to cement the parts of this our plan,
That all may hold.

F.   Meanwhile, go home and sleep
As honest men. My services will be

As great as any one of you will want ;
Yea, such the king himself would ask no more.

[*Exeunt.*

SCENE III.   *Night in the* High Sheriff's *office.*

High Sheriff. [*Writing*].   Gerard, Vowell, Henshaw,
      Finch, and—

Fox.   The rest
Not worth the ink that would inscribe their names.

H. S. These four are extra hot for this ?

F.   Hot as
The nether pit ; but two supply the fire.
Gerard and Vowell keep the others hot ;
And, having now a new incentive to
The work, they are aflame.

H. S.   Ah, ha !   What now ?

F. The callow king is offering knighthood, and
Five hundred pounds a year, to whosoe'er
Will take by steel, or lead, or potion given
In subtlety, the Lord Protector's life.

H. S. Knighthood indeed !   The darkest night
They ever saw, and Jack's hood o'er their skull,
With all the pounds of earth they need to keep
Their dust.   Thou know'st this for a verity ?

F. It came to us as tidings but to-night.
One Billingsley, a butcher, who is fag
For them, had read the document an hour
Before and packed the summary in
His pate.

H. S.   A miracle in duplicate.
The demons that were in the king flee at
The Lord Protector's name and enter swine :
To find as deep a sea as those of yore.
There is a diabolic something in
The name of Charles.   Belike, it is a word
That witches use to give a potence to

Their cabala ; and as an angle-worm,   ·
Cut through, makes two of one, so, when we kill
A Charles, we make another demon by
The trick.

    F.   From Gerard's privacy I filched
A precious secret, which was too esteemed
To flaunt before them all ; and though 'tis big
For one's belief to clasp, we may believe.
Rupert and envoy Baas are hand-and-glove
In this conspiracy.

    H. S.   What, Baas ! And is
The king of France a cut-throat with the rest ?
Methinks all kings are made of cursed stuff.
What proof hast thou of this ?

    F.   Gerard has proof ;
But it is kept, like sweetheart's hair, beside
His heart.

    H. S. We must have Gerard and his proof.
But tell the scope of their designs ; as well
The plans and means.

    F.   The scope includes the Lord
Protector's death and proclamation of
Young Charles ; the plan, to meet his lordship on
His usual ride, to-morrow morn ; the means,
With thirty troopers, and themselves, to do
The deed, then hie to London and proclaim
The king—the soldiers at the mews to be
Secured, and every gap be stopped through which
Might come mishap.

    H. S.   That spurs the ribs of our
Dispatch. To-night must give them warrant of
A holiday at common cost. Then shall
We hear how chuffly they will prate, when Death
Is thrumming hell-notes on their nerves, and see
How deftly they can carve out destinies
For royal vagabonds. Ere crows the cock

At broach of day no law of Clan Macduff,
Or other law to give their tether length,
Will lend a farthing's value to their lives.
But what is now the hour ? [*Looking at his watch.*]
          Near twelve o'clock ;
The hour for ghosts and rogues to disappear.
Seek thou thy bed ; and when the game is bagged
Prepare thyself to keep them company.

    F. When must I make confession of my part ?

    H. S. Before the judges.   Be thou sure to wear
A visage well veneered with penitence,
That men may deem it solid to the heart ;
And humor so thy voice that it shall have
A whipped-dog whine of sembled humbledness.
So shall Suspicion stand with bandaged eyes,
And thou wilt cheaply gain the guerdon of
Our great good will, and be as happy as
A man whose mother-in-law speaks well of him.
Of Billingsley and others thou canst give
Account another time. The leaders first,
In whom we get the priming ere the gun
Is fired. But time goes on, and we must go.   [*Exeunt.*]

    SCENE IV. CROMWELL *and the* High Sheriff *in a private
          room at Whitehall.*

    Cromwell. Have you this tumor ready for the lance ?

    High Sheriff. All the ringleaders are in custody,
With evidence in hand that Justice deems
Full twice enough to take their heads.   The rest
Are almost in our grasp.

    C.   Go on, and let
Them learn how far our hand can reach, until
The last one feels the gripe of vigilance—
Ay, to the lowest riff-raff of them all.

    H. S. The highest riff-raff gives the hardest task.

C. The greater pains to catch the greater gain
When caught. But nought must baffle you. No lord,
Encastled in the highest place, is high
Enough to mock the ladders of the law.

H. S. Suppose him nose-length off, but shielded by
A foreign arm.

C.　　　　There is no place for such
A supposition, since no foreign arm
Can shield a traitor here. Then nape the thought
And kick it from your mind into the street.

H. S. But what if we arouse the ire of France?

C. The ire of France! What ire has France to rouse?
She has no gag on me, no lien upon
The realm; nor can she claim a pennyworth
Of right this side her coast. Belike, some rogue
Has put his finger into our affairs;
Which insolent temerity shall not
Go unrebuked, though he be big enough
To personate all France, with half to spare.

H. S. Suppose we had indubitable proof
To implicate an envoy of the French
As in the league with Rupert, Gerard and
The rest?

C.　　　　Be Baas a miscreant such, he soon
Shall breathe his native air.

H. S.　　　　　　　　No less he is.

C. Then call him *base* who dare engage in aught
So base. An envoy full of envy at
Our peace; an envoy *extraordinary;*
An envoy come to play conspirator;
A serpent who would curse this Eden-isle!
The knave would pawn the honor of his king
To boot, and batten on his country's blood.
Knave? Search the Stygian depths of speech, **no word**
Is black enough to give the wretch a name.
Bring him upon the ready foot of haste,

To try our scalpel on his impudence.
But first your proof.

  H. S.   There is sufficient there.

            [*Handing a letter.*

  C. [*Reading*]. Where got you this?

  H. S.   In Sir John Gerard's pocket.

  C. A pockey pocket—like to give them all
The pocks they want. What other proofs have you?

  H. S. That letter quickened assiduity
And set us on the path between the two.
Fox was despatched, beneath the night's disguise,
To try his craft ere yet the envoy knew
Of what had happed. He met De Baas alone ;
Spoke of the letter, which was owned ; and, though
The Frenchman calked his speech with caution, he,
By subtlety, compelled a leak, and found
Him cognizant that they designed you ill.
At Rupert's name his taciturnity
Forgot itself, betraying knowledge of
A plan that ramifies the continent,
In unofficial guise, at which the kings
Are pleased to wink, while wishing at God-speed.
That plan includes your death, a vacant throne,
And Charles, the royal vagabond, restored.

  C. A fellow-feeling for a fellow-king
Breeds coward wishes for a coward work ;
For none of them, nor all, dare shew the hand.
What kingliness, that their puissances
Are clinging to Assassination's arm !
What phantom majesty, that vanishes
When honor calls for common manliness !
What idols these for nations to adore !
What incarnations of divinity—
To sprawl in hell-slime foul as this ! See that
You trace this plot, as from a river's mouth ;
Yea, up its tributaries, even should

It take you up to mountain sources and
The highest springs. I want Malignancy
To see our vigilance and feel our power.
 H. S. Scant gleaning waits, I ween ; but I will glean.
  [*Exit H. S. Cromwell goes to the council chamber.*
 Lord Chief Justice. What is the pleasure of your high-
  ness in
The case of Gerard, Vowell, Fox, *et al.?*
 C. Let justice make the leaders feel our hand ;
While mercy does a justice to our heart,
By shaking but a warning at the rest,
To make them shake. Then send them forth ; and as
They find the law's black ear-mark on their names,
So will their mordant memory fix it in
Their fears. Our strength advertised thus, will hint
To Treason not to leave his lurking-place.   ·
Gerard and Vowell, then, must get their dues,
To shew that mercy can discriminate ;
While Fox, who does full credit to his name,
May have a hole provided for escape.
 L. C. J. Your mercy leaves but little to the law.
Justice was never cheated so before.
 C. I would not be as that poor relic of
A king who backs these villains, having too
Great poverty of soul for one good deed.
I would not have his cowardice, to strike
From 'twixt the bars of my security.
I would not hurt a brute save to escape
Its hurt. Far liefer would I mercy got
The better of the law than law of mercy,
Which oft is stronger, better than the law.
'Tis wife to justice, having woman's heart,
Tempering the rigor of her lord's decrees.
'Tis hers to yield obedience, his to love.
Yet she in serving more than half controls.
 L. C. J. You treat your foes less ill than Charles his
  friends.

C. Hence foes become my friends, and friends his
    foes.   [*Exit L. C. J.*
Usher. The envoy of the French is here.
C.   Admit.

Enter DE BAAS.

Baas. Your honored servant hasted at the word
To learn your highness' will, in hope to find
Assured continued amity between
This realm and that I humbly represent.

C. Is treason like to give us amity ?

B. There is no treason in my master's heart.

C. Thy treason were enough for fifty hearts.

B. Your highness shocks me with unusual speech.

C. And thou hast shocked us with unusual deeds.

B. Pardon, your highness. I am from a court
Whose king has reverence for your worthy parts.
I saw him stand before your portrait, as
Before the grandeur of a mountain, lost
In thought.

C.   As thou art lost in honesty,
Which is as far from thee as thou art short
Of heaven. But tut, thou milk-and-honey tongue !
Not of thy master but of thee I spoke.

B. A most unworthy servant, I admit ;
And yet a servant who would serve him well,
Nor in my serving do your highness ill.

C. 'Twere well thy heart were truthful as thy lip.

B. My heart is in my royal master's work.

C. What is it then that meddles so with mine ?

B. The duties of my office claim of me
Some knowledge of the court with which it is
My mission to—

C.   Thy mission ! Prythee, is
Thy mission to collude with traitors ? to
Abet the bloody cowardice of the
Assassin ? to attempt to overthrow

The government to which thy mission is ?
Is that thy mission for thy master here ?

B. Nay, pardon me, your worthy highness, if,
Through an unworthy word or doubtful deed,
Occasion gives excuse for what you say ;
But never have I thought to do you wrong.

    C. Then Satan must have formed thy thoughts of
      right.

Look thou at that [*Handing the letter*], and thou wilt
    hear thyself
Called liar by thyself.

    B.   Mary Mother !
Oh, what a plot is this !

    C.   Ay, plot indeed !
And thou neck deep in it. Yet hast thou had
No thought of wrong !

    B.   A plot, I mean, to do
Me fatal wrong.

    C.   Thee wrong ! Heaven could not do
The wrong by barring every gate against
Thy entrance ; neither hell, though it should plunge
Thee head first in its liquid flames. Then how
Shall earth ?

    B.   This letter is not mine.

    C.   In that
Thou sayest what is true, yet liest with
The truth ; for now it is not thine, though thine
It was before it left thy hand.

    B.   Mother
Of God ! but I am innocent.

    C.   The God
Who was before the mother was will call
Thee to account for this. Pray what is guilt
If thou be innocent ? Why, hell itself would bite
The lip ere vouching for thy innocence.
If thou be innocent, we need not rail

At sin. If thou be innocent, Satan
Must be a saint. If thou be innocent,
There is no use for hell.

  B.   You have a knave's
Device against my word, and trust the knave
Instead of me, who am the servant of
An august king.

  C.   Ay, knave indeed—thyself
The knave ; and now a double knave. It is
That knave I trust against this knave. Prank not
Thyself upon our lack of proof, to back
The black-and-white that stares thee in the face.
We have such telltales that, if summoned as
The ghosts of sin which haunt men's consciences,
Their burning hands would slap thee on the mouth
And blister thee.

  B.   In rating me it is
Not me your highness rates, but France.

  C.   What ! would'st
Thou add a coward to a knave, and smutch
Thy country's name to save thyself ? Go, wretch,
And face the country thou would'st thus defame !
Go, tell thy master of thy faithlessness,
And thank him that his friendship saves thy head.
For hadst thou got thy dues, the laws, by this,
Had laid thy lying tongue at lasting rest,
And rid the land of one who proves its bane.
Go, then, nor leave thy footprints on the shore ;
And tell that Cromwell lives in spite of thee—
In spite of all the spawn that hell can spare—
While England flourishes as ne'er before.

THE END.

www.ingramcontent.com/pod-product-compliance
Lightning Source LLC
Chambersburg PA
CBHW020008030726
47500CB00002B/502